Only ~~one time~~ Forever

D.E. Haggerty

Also by D.E. Haggerty

My Forever Love

Forever For You

Just For Forever

Stay For Forever

Meet Disaster

Meet Not

Meet Dare

Meet Hate

Bragg's Truth

Bragg's Love

Perfect Bragg

Bragg's Match

Bragg's Christmas

How to Date a Rockstar

How to Love a Rockstar

How to Fall For a Rockstar

How to be a Rockstar's Girlfriend

How to Catch a Rockstar

Before It Was Love

After The Vows

While We Waited
A Hero for Hailey
A Protector for Phoebe
A Soldier for Suzie
A Fox for Faith
A Christmas for Chrissie
A Valentine for Valerie
A Love for Lexi
About Face
At Arm's Length
Hands Off
Knee Deep
Molly's Misadventures

Chapter 1

Patience – the capacity to tolerate a grumpy boss without wanting to throw him in a steaming pile of burning biomass

"Lilac!"

At the sound of my boss, Beckett, bellowing my name throughout the office, I close my eyes and search for patience.

"Lilac!"

The second bellow of my name makes it clear today will not be the day I discover the ability to accept my boss' interruptions without becoming annoyed, although no one will notice my annoyance. On the outside, I'm completely composed.

I'm always composed. My sisters believe I have no emotions. Just because I don't fling my emotions at random passers-by the way they do doesn't mean I don't have any. There's no reason to inflict my emotional baggage on other people. I don't want theirs, why would they want mine?

I inhale a deep breath and let it out slowly before I rise from my chair. I run a hand down my skirt to smooth away the wrinkles caused by hours of sitting before exiting my office and walking to Beckett's.

I frown when I notice the empty desk in front of his office. His personal assistant should be sitting here. If she were at her desk, he wouldn't feel the need to yell my name throughout the building.

"Where's Brandi?" I ask upon entering my boss' office.

"How should I know?"

Is he serious?

"Because she's your PA and she could summon people into your office using this handy device known as a telephone allowing you to save your yelling and screaming for your private life."

A hint of humor flares in his eyes before he blinks, and it's gone. I wish I could say the hint doesn't make my belly feel warm and tingly, but I do not lie. It's not that I don't have the ability to lie. Nearly everyone has the ability to lie. I simply choose not to.

Beckett clears his throat and despite knowing the likelihood of whatever he's planning to say angering me, I can't help myself from anticipating the sound of his voice. His voice is deep and gravely. It's on the top of the long list detailing the reasons why the man is the sexiest person I've ever met.

Next on the list is his face. Combine his deep blue eyes, high cheekbones, and square jaw and all the standard requirements for sexy have been not only met but exceeded. It would be a perfect face except his nose is a bit too straight and there's a small bump in the middle of it as if it's been broken in the past. If he didn't spend all his time barking at me, I'd ask him what happened.

I mustn't forget to mention his hair, which also makes the top ten of the list. It's thick and dark except when the sun shines and streaks of blond become visible. Those streaks along with the curl at his neck give him a careless, youthful appearance despite his age of thirty-eight.

If his sexy voice and almost perfect face weren't enough to cause flutters in my belly, his body could do the job all on its own. I'm quite tall for a woman at five-foot-nine and Beckett at an even six-foot is the perfect size for me. Not too tall, but not too short either.

He also spends a great deal of time working out causing his biceps to strain at the sleeves of his button-down tops. Men who work out a great deal can quickly become disproportional with overdeveloped neck muscles and underdeveloped quadriceps, but Beckett's body is the perfect balance.

"I don't scream," he protests, and my contemplation of his sexiness comes to a complete halt.

I raise an eyebrow and cross my arms over my chest. There's no need to speak. He knows very well he was screaming since my office is down the hall from his and yet I heard him perfectly.

"How did your meeting with the White Bridge city administrators go? Are they interested in our firm helping to improve their recycling?"

At his question, I enjoy a moment of imagining myself strangling him. Not to death. Just enough to cause him to lose the ability to speak for a while.

I'm not a violent person. I would never actually strangle him, but I read an article suggesting imagining the act as a way to cope with frustration with a person. An article I only read because Beckett is the most frustrating person I've ever met.

Although his question seems appropriate enough – I did meet with the city administrators today to discuss their recycling program – it's not. Before Beckett arrived and took over the CEO position at *Clean Mountain Environment* last year, I had complete autonomy over my work.

"I'm nearly finished with the report. I'll have it on your desk by tomorrow morning."

He growls in annoyance, and my stomach dips at the sound. Beckett Dempsey may be the most frustrating man on the planet, but his sexy growls make me want to do wicked things to him *and* with him.

No, Lilac. Those thoughts are highly inappropriate. Beckett Dempsey is your boss. You do not want to do wicked things with him. It's the sexual frustration speaking. Ever since Beckett showed up, I haven't had any time to meet with a sexual partner.

I frown. Sexual partner? Considering it's been months since I had sex, I think it's safe to say I no longer have any sexual partners. Damn Beckett.

"I don't want to wait for the report. I want to know what the city administrators said from you. Now," he grits out between clenched teeth.

I don't know why he's angry. He has no right to be angry. I'm the one who should be angry. He's questioning my work. No one questions my work.

"I'll get my report," I say and pivot on my heel to march out of the room.

"You can—"

I ignore the rest of whatever he says. If I don't get out of his office as soon as possible, I'm going to kill him. I know killing's wrong, but if anyone can get away with murder, it's me. I know numerous ways to make his death appear to be an accident.

Alternatively, I can dispose of the body in such a way as to ensure it's never found again. The biomass project I'm working on in my hometown of Winter Falls would be a perfect place. No. I shut those thoughts down. I can't corrupt the project with a human body. Besides, the project isn't ready yet.

The mere fact I'm contemplating corrupting my project is an indication of how strong my anger is. How dare Beckett question my work? Who does he think he is?

I am aware he is the CEO of *Clean Mountain Environment* and technically my 'boss', but I maintain I don't need a boss. I've been working at the environmental engineering firm ever since I completed my master's degree eight years ago. I've proven myself to be an independent worker who finishes her projects on time – if not ahead of time – with hardly any complaint from customers.

I print the report – in triplicate as you never know how many copies you'll need – and save it on an external device as well before returning to Beckett's office.

I place the items on his desk. "Here you are. If there's nothing else…," I trail off as I make my way to the door.

"Hold up," he says, and I stop a mere footstep away from the door. "I want to discuss your recommendations to the city."

He wants to discuss my recommendations? Is he questioning my work? How dare he!

I should quit. I don't need the aggravation this man causes in my life. He telephones and messages me at all times of the day and night as if it's his right and interrupts my personal life with questions that could easily be answered during working hours. Ever since he became the CEO, my work-life balance has disappeared.

Do not misunderstand me. I love my job. I love my chosen field of work. I don't mind working extra hours. I have no problem with the work portion of my work-life balance being on the heavier side. I do have a problem with not having control of how the balance is maintained.

Unfortunately, quitting isn't my best option. *Clean Mountain Environment* is the only environmental engineering firm within driving distance of my hometown of Winter Falls. Unless I want to relocate – and I don't – I have to persevere with Beckett as my boss.

"Perhaps it would be more helpful if you read my report and my recommendations first," I suggest to the door since I can't turn around without it being perfectly clear to my boss how pissed off I am at this moment.

"Come sit down," he orders. "You can explain your recommendations to me in person instead of me having to read a boring report."

I bristle. My report is anything but boring. It outlines the numerous avenues White Bridge can pursue to improve their recycling program and how we can assist them with this endeavor.

While I realize this type of work sounds boring to the majority of people, I maintain it's fascinating. Growing up in Winter Falls – the first carbon neutral town in the world – gave me an appreciation of the environment and how important it is. Inventing creative ways to save it is invigorating.

I inhale a deep breath and count to ten before letting it out. The action doesn't calm me – at least, not completely – but it is enough to smooth out the anger in my face.

"I didn't realize you needed my help understanding recycling," I say as I sit down across from him.

He chuckles and his blue eyes sparkle. "Good thing you're here to help me then."

I frown. He isn't supposed to be amused. He should be offended.

"If you don't understand recycling methods, you shouldn't be the CEO," I tell him.

The humor disappears. "Do not question my competency," he growls.

My core trembles at his growl and I cross my legs to relieve some of the growing tension. Beckett's eyes drop to my legs. When his gaze returns to my face, heat is evident in his eyes. I want to run away before I lose control of my sexual desire for him, but I quash the impulse. Running away won't improve the situation.

I must continue to maintain strict control over my emotions. My sexual desire is immaterial as he believes I'm incompetent. I will never spend time on a man who thinks I don't know how to do my job. Besides, he's my boss. Work relationships are statistically doomed to fail.

Even if such a relationship weren't doomed from the start, working with someone you're personally involved in is complicated, and I don't do complicated.

Chapter 2

Scheming – when sisters make underhand plans that scare the pants off of men

BECKETT

I slow my car as I reach the *Welcome to Winter Falls* sign. What am I doing here? Why can't I leave Lilac alone?

No matter how many times I tell myself to stop bothering her, I can't. And now she hasn't responded to any of my messages for a day. Is she okay? Is she in trouble? Has something happened to her?

My heart rate accelerates at the idea of her being in danger. I need to make sure there's nothing wrong. I need to know she's not in trouble.

I check my rearview mirror and my heart rate accelerates for an entirely different reason. A cop car is flashing its lights at me. I check my speedometer, but I'm driving the speed limit. His siren begins to wail, and I pull to the side of the road.

I roll down my window and wait as the police officer makes his way to my car. I force a smile on my face as I ask, "How can I help you today, Officer?"

I know better than to ask why he's pulling me over. Police officers do not appreciate having their actions questioned. Even thinking of how I know that makes my hands curl into the steering wheel until my knuckles turn white.

"Where are you going?"

My brow wrinkles. "Where am I going?" I repeat, because I'm confused. What does it matter to him where I'm going? It's not illegal to drive on a road in a town in Colorado.

"Yes. Where are you going in Winter Falls?" he speaks slowly as if I'm an idiot.

"I'm here to see Lilac West," I answer despite thinking it's none of his damn business who I'm here to visit.

"Lilac?" He grins. "Phew. What a relief. I thought the gossip gals would set their sights on me next."

Gossip gals? Sights? What the hell is he talking about?

"Pardon?"

He waves away my question with a flick of his hand. "Don't worry about it." He extends his hand. "I'm Peace."

"Peace?" I ask as we shake hands. "Your name is Peace and you're a peace officer?"

"Yep. Mom thought if she gave me the name Peace, I'd be a well-behaved child." He smirks. "She couldn't have been more wrong."

I sympathize with his poor mom. I raised my four sisters after our parents passed away. I love those four girls more than anything in the world but raising them was by far the most difficult thing I've ever done in my life.

"I'm sure you gave her a run for her money," I murmur.

"I did." He knocks on the hood and strolls away.

I reach forward to switch on the engine, but he returns. "Oops. Sorry. I forgot to write you a ticket."

"Write me a ticket? What was I doing wrong?"

"Gasoline engine vehicles are illegal in Winter Falls."

I open my mouth to tell him my car isn't a gasoline engine before I remember I'm driving my sister's car since she 'borrowed' mine. Without asking mind you. Cassandra doesn't let things like asking permission get in her way.

"They are? How the hell do people get around?"

"Bikes and golf carts."

I nod. It makes sense. And, as the CEO of an environmental engineering company, I can appreciate how their efforts benefit the earth. But there's one problem with their approach.

"How do I actually get into town?" They can't expect me to drive the thirty miles from my home in White Bridge to Winter Falls in a golf cart. It would destroy all the good their policy is trying to do.

Peace scratches his beard. "Oh yeah. You're not from here. You can park your car at the lot next to the *Inn on Main*. There are golf carts you can borrow available there."

"Thanks." I guess this means I'm not getting a ticket. I don't ask him, though. No sense reminding him of why he pulled me over.

"I'll see you at the party."

"Wait!" I call before he can walk away. "What party?"

"For Lilac's sister's moving-in party."

Lilac has a sister? She never told me.

"Where's the party?"

"At Maverick Langston's house."

Maverick Langston? As in the movie star, Maverick Langston? He lives in the town of Winter Falls? What else has Lilac been hiding from me?

"I'll give you a ride," he says and marches back to his patrol vehicle before I can ask him any further questions.

After we drop my car off at the lot, I hop into the patrol vehicle with Peace. We're quiet as he drives us to a large colonial house. The street in front is crowded with golf carts and the front yard is littered with bikes. I guess he wasn't kidding about the no cars policy.

When I open the car door, the sound of laughter and music hits me. It's a party all right.

"Come on. Everyone's in back." He indicates I should follow him as we round the house into the backyard.

Quiet falls when we arrive. Why is everyone quiet all of a sudden? Is someone going to make an announcement? I scan the area and realize everyone's staring at me. I understand I'm a stranger here, but it's no reason to stare.

The crowd opens up and there she is. Lilac 'pain in my ass' West. The tension in my body slips away as I realize she's okay. She's perfectly fine and hasn't been in the horrific accident I'd imagined.

As I watch, she scowls and stomps her way across the lawn toward me. Even scowling, Lilac West is the most beautiful woman I've ever seen. Her hair is a light brown color with streaks of blonde running through it. It's long enough for me to fist in my hand while I plunder her mouth with those pouty pink lips.

Her brown eyes are the color of my favorite whisky. They're also sharp and don't miss a thing. The freckles scattered across her nose and cheeks lessen the hardness of her features and make her appear younger than the thirty years I know her to be.

"What are you doing here?" she asks when she reaches me.

"I was about to ask you the same thing."

"You have no right to ask about my whereabouts when it's not related to work."

"When you refused to answer my messages, I assumed you were on a date." I spit the word date out of my mouth.

A couple of weeks after I arrived at *Clean Mountain Environment*, I asked Lilac to join me for lunch. She said no without an explanation. I found out the reason on my own when I saw her entering a local hotel with a man. And it wasn't the last time I saw her at a hotel with a man either.

Because Lilac West is a player, which is a shame since she's also my ideal woman. Smart, serious about her work, doesn't take crap from anyone – including me – and gorgeous to top it all off.

"I refused to answer your calls because I am not at your beck and call despite what you may believe."

I know she's not at my beck and call but whose beck and call is she at?

"You rushed out of the office in a hurry yesterday. I thought there was a problem."

She crosses her arms over her chest, and I force my gaze to remain on her eyes. I don't need to look down to know the movement caused her breasts to press together. The vision has been seared into my brain since the first time I saw it.

"I did not rush out of the office. I completed my tasks for the day and left."

"You didn't check with me before leaving."

Her nostrils flare. "I didn't realize checking with you was a requirement before leaving for the day."

"Go get him, Lilac!" A woman encourages from behind her.

I glance past her and notice a tall, blonde woman waving at me. "Who is she?"

"She is none of your business. My private life is none of your business. I concede you are my boss."

I snort. "How gracious of you."

"But being my boss does not entitle you to information about my private life. I'd prefer it if you left now."

The woman skips over to us. "Hi." She holds out her hand. "I'm Ashlyn."

I reach forward to shake her hand. She latches onto my hand and drags me further into the yard. "We're having a party. Come join us. I'll introduce you to everyone."

I glance back at Lilac over my shoulder. She's glaring at Ashlyn. I can't help the smile from creeping onto my face. Annoying Lilac is one of my favorite things in the world.

Ashlyn leads me to a group of women. "This is Aspen." A woman with dark, curly hair waves. "And this is Ellery." A short woman with reddish-blonde hair nods to me. "Our other sister, Juniper, is still in the house."

Sister? I cock an eyebrow. "You're all sisters of Lilac's?"

Ashlyn giggles. "Lilac didn't tell you about us?"

"Lilac doesn't share her private life with me," I mutter under my breath.

"Interesting," Aspen says.

Ellery wags her finger at her. "Don't. Leave Lilac alone. Don't interfere. You'll make things worse."

What things will she make worse? What are they talking about? I know from having four sisters, women have a secret language men are bound to never understand.

"I thought we agreed. Lilac's next," Aspen says.

"Just because she doesn't have a man doesn't mean it's her turn," Ellery argues.

"Lilac has a man," I point out. More than one, I think but know better than to say.

The sisters look at each other. They don't speak, but I'm certain they're having some kind of private conversation only they can understand. They seem to come to some sort of understanding before turning to me.

Aspen grins. "This is going to be fun."

"We need to get the betting pools set up," Ashlyn says.

"Can we at least wait until Juniper and Maverick come out before we start on the next one?" Ellery's question does nothing to clear up the confusion their conversation is causing.

"I think I should go," I say as I begin backing away.

"But you haven't met Juniper yet," Ashlyn argues.

"Another time," I mumble and then high-tail it out of there.

I know the look of scheming sisters and those sisters are definitely scheming about something. Besides, I don't need to be here. I came to check on Lilac. She's obviously fine and doesn't want me here. My mission here is complete.

I scan the yard until my gaze falls on Lilac. She's glaring at me with her hands fisted at her hips. Her obvious anger does nothing to distract from her beauty. It doesn't matter. I can't get involved with the woman. Not only is she my employee, but she's a player. I know better than to get involved with a player.

Chapter 3

Sisters – trouble whether or not you're related to them by blood

As I walk down the hallway at work on Monday morning while studying a soil report on my tablet, the hair on the back of my neck prickles. Unfortunately, I've become intimately acquainted with this feeling over the past year and know exactly what it means. Beckett Dempsey is approaching. I peek up from beneath my eyelashes and, sure enough, he's prowling his way toward me.

I've had about enough of Beckett Dempsey and his interfering ways. Who does he think he is? It's bad enough he believes me to be incompetent, but now he's invading my hometown because he thinks I'm avoiding him? My hometown is my sanctuary. He doesn't belong there.

I duck into the restroom before Beckett can reach me. I set my tablet on the counter and splash cold water on my wrists. Despite the lack of scientific evidence confirming cold water on wrists cools a body down, the water feels refreshing.

I stare at myself in the mirror and discover my cheeks are flushed and my eyes are dilated. I glare at my face. I am not sexually aroused by Beckett. The vision in the mirror calls me a liar. I frown. I am not a slave to my body.

I don't care how attractive Beckett is or how much my body yearns for his. I will never act on those yearnings. He's my boss. Getting mixed up with him would hurt my career and my career is the most important thing in my life. I can find my boss sexually attractive and continue to work with him in a professional manner.

Bang! Bang! Bang!

"I know you're in there, Lilac," Beckett yells through the door.

My lips purse. He may not act professional toward me, but I will not stoop to his level. No matter how incompetent he thinks I am.

"Beckett!" a woman shouts. "What are you doing? Trying to break the door to the woman's room down?"

I know the voice. It's Cassandra, Beckett's sister.

"I'm merely—"

"Don't make me summon HR on you, old man."

"I'm not an old man. I'm thirty-eight."

"As I said. Old man. Now, get on out of here. I thought as the big, bad, important CEO you'd have more important things to do than breaching the restroom."

The door flies open and three women – Cassandra, Elizabeth, and Gabrielle – tromp into the room. They're Beckett's sisters. None of whom work at *Clean Mountain Environment*, although they don't hesitate to visit their brother here on a regular basis.

"Were you hiding from Beckett in the bathroom?" Cassandra asks without bothering to greet me.

Gabrielle gasps and widens her eyes at Cassandra's behavior.

"You can't ask her that kind of question," Elizabeth admonishes.

Cassandra shrugs. "Why not?"

"It's rude," Gabrielle says in a barely audible voice. Beckett's youngest sister is incredibly shy.

"Exactly," Elizabeth agrees.

Cassandra rolls her eyes. "Who cares? How am I going to get the skinny on what's going on with Beckett if I'm afraid to ask the hard questions?"

"And here everyone says I'm the awkward one and yet you're the one using slang from the 80s," Elizabeth claims.

I clear my throat. "Actually, the phrase 'getting the skinny on someone' stems from World War II."

Cassandra giggles. "Why am I not surprised Beckett fell for a woman who knows the history of the phrase 'get the skinny on'?"

"Beckett hasn't fallen for me. Quite the contrary. He thinks I'm incompetent."

Gabrielle's eyes widen and she shuffles closer. "Is he… is he." She clears her throat. "Is he mean to you?"

I study her. Based on her actions today and past interactions I've had with her, I hypothesize she's suffered at the hands of a man in the past. Although, I find it difficult to believe Beckett would ever let anyone harm one of his sisters.

As much as the man irritates me, I can't deny he's a good brother. He practically raised his siblings after their parents passed when he was in his late teens. He must have done something right as three of his four sisters followed him to Colorado when he took over the CEO position here at *Clean Mountain Environment.*

I don't want Gabrielle to think her brother is an asshole no matter how much I wish I could strangle him at times. "He's not unkind."

Cassandra bursts out laughing. "No, he's grumpy and annoying."

I can't disagree with her assessment. Usually, I prefer not to use the word grumpy as it's too colloquial and ambiguous, but, in this case, it fits. Beckett is a grump.

Bang! Bang! Bang!

"Are you having a convention in there?" Beckett asks.

"Yep!" Cassandra exclaims. "We're having a convention about women's hygiene products. Which do you prefer – pads or tampons?"

Gabrielle blushes and drops her chin to her chest until her hair covers her face.

"You can't scare me away with talk of tampons. Do you not remember who went to the store to buy your feminine hygiene products when you were teenagers?"

"He bought everything in the female hygiene aisle," Elizabeth fills me in. "We had boxes and boxes of pads in our bathroom. I used them to stuff my bra." Her eyes widen when she realizes what she said, and she slaps a hand over her mouth.

Cassandra elbows her. "Amateur. I took boxes of tampons with me to school and used them to make candles in shop class."

"How do you make candles from tampons?" I ask.

"You dip them in hot wax and light them on fire."

"And then she threw them in the boy's locker room," Elizabeth says.

"You remind me of my sister, Ashlyn," I tell her.

Elizabeth smirks. "Ashlyn must be awesome."

She is, but I have no intention of ever admitting to my sister what I think of her. My baby sister does not need anyone encouraging her. Encouraging her only leads to more outrageous behavior.

"You told me you weren't responsible for starting the fire in the boy's room," Beckett says as he bursts into the restroom. I guess he became tired of waiting in the hallway for us.

Cassandra winks at him. "Technically, I didn't start the fire. The boys started the fire when they threw the tampons into the garbage can before they extinguished the flames."

"You girls give me gray hair," he mumbles.

"What gray hair? You're as handsome as you've always been. Don't you agree, Lilac?"

I glare at Cassandra. I hate to lie. I believe in telling the truth at all times. Lies and false information are bad. And I do mean bad in the worst way imaginable. Spreading false information can literally start wars and has in the past.

I settle for evasion. A tactic I'm loathe to employ. It's nearly as bad as misinformation.

"Beckett is my boss. I believe it's inappropriate to discuss the attractiveness of your boss in the workplace."

Beckett smirks. "As inappropriate as it is to discuss tampons in the ladies' room?"

I know he's referring to Cassandra's fire incident, but I can pretend better than my sisters give me credit for. "I believe the ladies' room is exactly the place women should discuss tampons."

"You shouldn't be in here," Gabrielle says.

"Why not?" Beckett asks.

Her gaze drops to the floor. "Women should feel comfortable in here."

Beckett's brow knits as he studies his sister. "I'll go. I don't want anyone to feel uncomfortable."

He starts for the door, but Cassandra laces her arm through his before he can make it there. "We'll all go. Come on. Beckett's treating us to lunch."

When I remain standing, she motions for me to follow her. "You too, Lilac."

I check my watch. "It's not time for lunch yet."

"The boss can't tattle on you when you're with him." She winks.

"I'm not concerned about the boss. I'm concerned about finishing my work on time."

Beckett halts. "Are you going to miss a deadline?"

I lock my jaw to keep myself from lashing out at him. I have never missed a deadline. He should know this. Instead, he continues to question my work time and time again. I am the most competent environmental engineer at the company, but he acts as if I graduated college yesterday and have never successfully completed a project.

"I don't miss deadlines, because I don't sneak off for lunch at 11 a.m.," I respond in a calm voice despite my desire to throw my tablet at him.

"We're not sneaking," Cassandra claims.

"Because someone's got too big of a mouth to sneak anywhere," Elizabeth says.

Cassandra stops and props her fists on her hips. "I'll have you know I snuck out of the house just fine when we were going up."

Beckett groans. "Stop. I don't want to know. All of you survived." He briefly glances at Gabrielle before continuing. "And you are functioning adults now. Let's not re-hash the past."

"You don't want to hear about the time I snuck out and went to a Pearl Jam concert?"

He pinches his nose. "No, I do not."

I cough to cover up my laugh. Seeing Beckett frustrated is worth a few awkward moments in the restroom with his sisters.

"Have a nice lunch," I say as I leave to return to my office.

"Lilac," Beckett calls. I stop but don't glance back. "I'll drop in after lunch to discuss your deadlines."

I nod because it's impossible to speak with my teeth clenched together. I wait until I'm certain they're gone before I stomp to my office.

I throw my tablet on my desk before closing my eyes and counting to ten. Once I reach ten, I continue until twenty. I give up when I've counted to one hundred. There's no calming down after Beckett basically said he doesn't believe I will meet my deadlines.

I have done nothing but work my ass off for this company. What have I ever done to make Beckett believe I'm incompetent?

Chapter 4

Get 'you' sorted – an excuse sisters use to invade your home and steal your beer

"WE'RE HERE!" ASHLYN EXCLAIMS as she along with my other sisters – Aspen, Ellery, and Juniper – invade my one-bedroom apartment.

"There's no need to announce yourself. A herd of elephants would have been quieter," I chastise.

"Elephants are actually usually quiet," Juniper says. She's an animal lover and has a vast array of knowledge about them making her position as manager of the Wildlife Refuge outside of town the perfect job for her.

"I didn't think you noticed our grand entrance since your head was buried in your laptop," Ashlyn says.

"It's impossible to bury your head in a laptop. I hope you know this."

"It's Friday night. Why aren't you at the bar drinking?" my oldest sister, Aspen, asks.

My brow furrows. I'm never at the bar drinking on Friday night unless they drag me there. They know this.

"Yeah. I thought I was the workaholic in the family," Ellery adds before she plops down on my sofa.

If anyone in the family can compete with me with regard to the number of hours worked in a week, it's Ellery. She runs the *Inn on Main* and practically works from sunrise to sunset. Or, rather, she used to. Now she has an adorable baby daughter and a fiancé to spend her time with.

"No, you're the stubborn one," Aspen tells Ellery.

"Me?" Ellery points to herself. "I'm not the one who—"

"Nope," Aspen cuts her off. "We don't discuss the ancient past."

Ellery's referring to when Aspen believed her high school sweetheart, Lyric, betrayed her causing her to abandon Winter Falls for a decade. She had no choice but to return to our hometown last summer when her bookstore and apartment in Dallas burnt down.

Since then, she's rekindled her love affair with Lyric and the two are now engaged. I'm happy for her, but I do not approve of how she's nominated herself to be the family matchmaker since Lyric put his ring on her finger.

"You don't have any beer in your refrigerator," Ashlyn remarks from the kitchen where she's searching the appliance.

"You shouldn't be drinking. You're pregnant. Drinking alcohol while pregnant causes—"

She slams the refrigerator shut and shoves her palm in my face. "No. You don't get to lecture me about what I can and cannot do as a pregnant woman."

"Why not?" Ellery asks. "Everyone thought they could tell me what to do when I was pregnant with Willow."

"Oh please." Ashlyn rolls her eyes. "You hid your pregnancy from the entire town for the first two trimesters whereas everyone in town has known I'm pregnant since the second the line appeared on the stick."

"Because you told everyone," Ellery reminds her.

Ellery is correct. Ashlyn eloped to marry Rowan, the man she has loved since high school, before Christmas, and by Easter she was pregnant. I realized she was pregnant straight away as I did with Ellery. But unlike with my older sister, who wanted to keep her condition a secret, my youngest sister tells everyone who will listen about how she's 'knocked up'.

"I could use a beer," Juniper says as she collapses on the sofa next to Ellery.

"Why do you need a beer? Is your handsome movie star fiancé keeping you up late every night?" Ashlyn waggles her eyebrows.

"I'm not engaged to Maverick. We barely moved in together."

Ashlyn waves away Juniper's comment. "You'll be engaged soon enough. Word on the street has it he wanted to propose last weekend when you moved in with him."

"The gossip gals are the bane of my existence," Juniper mutters.

I have to agree with my sister in this regard. The gossip gals are five elderly women in Winter Falls who have made it their mission in life to know every single piece of gossip in town. It's impossible to keep a secret when they're around. And they're always around.

Aspen claps. "We didn't come here to discuss Juniper's love life. She's sorted."

Juniper snorts. "Gee, thanks, big sis."

Aspen ignores her to continue. "We came here to get Lilac sorted."

Ellery raises her hand. "I came here to get a break from a screaming baby. Don't get me wrong. I love Willow with every beat of my heart, but she's an asshole when she has colic."

"Have you tried—"

"Yes!" Ellery shouts. "I have tried everything you can imagine for a baby with colic. Pacifier, hikes in her stroller, rocking her, swaddling her…the list goes on and on. I don't need you – my motherless sister – to lecture me on how to deal with a baby."

I lift an eyebrow. Ellery doesn't usually lose her temper. She's stubborn, but she doesn't have much of a temper.

Her shoulders deflate as she lets out of huff of air. "I'm sorry. This no sleeping with a baby stuff is tough."

"I hope my baby sleeps through the night," Ashlyn says as she rubs her belly. "I have other things to do in the night than rock a baby if you get what I'm saying."

Juniper grunts. "The astronauts on the International Space Station caught your sexual innuendo."

"If everyone's finished discussing babies, can we get to the reason for this evening's adventure now?" Aspen growls.

As the oldest sister of the West family, Aspen's pushy but she doesn't usually growl at people. My brow wrinkles as I study her. Something is up with her. Two possibilities come immediately to mind. One, she's upset she's not yet married to Lyric. Or, two, she's trying to get pregnant and has yet to be successful.

Based on her annoyance with the baby talk, I hypothesize she's trying to get pregnant. This is mere supposition, however. I'll need to observe her closer for factual indicators before I can make a proper conclusion.

"There's no need to 'get Lilac sorted' as you so eloquently put it." I have no chance of changing the topic once Aspen has put on her matchmaker hat, but it's worth a try.

"Beep!" Ashlyn pretends to push a buzzer. "Wrong. We want all the deets on Beckett."

"I told you everything there is to know about Beckett. He's the CEO of *Clean Mountain Environment* and as such my boss. There is nothing more to tell."

"Lilac. Lilac. Lilac." Aspen tsks at me. "There's obviously more to the story. He didn't show up at Juniper's moving-in party for nothing."

"And left before I got a chance to meet him," Juniper whines.

"Hold up. I have a picture." Ashlyn digs her phone out of her pocket and unlocks it before handing it to Juniper.

"Yowzah. Mr. CEO is a hottie."

"For sure," Ashlyn says as she puts her phone away. "I'd totally add him to my spank bank if I wasn't married to a former

NFL quarterback who can bake like a dream and is the star of all my wet dreams."

"Ahem! We all agree Beckett is attractive, can we discuss another topic now?" The very last thing I need is my sisters reminding me of how attractive my boss is. It's difficult enough to forget as it is.

"Personally, I think Cole's more attractive. Beckett is too big and burly for me. I prefer a leaner man," Ellery says.

"Two cheers for leaner men!" Juniper raises her hand and they high-five.

"Anyway, we've given you a few days since the party. Time's up." Aspen motions for me to proceed. Proceed with what is the question.

I purse my lips. "What are you referring to? Why is my time up?" My sisters are baffling at times.

She rolls her eyes. "Beckett wants you. What are you going to do about it? Are you going to jump in bed with him? Are you going to make him work for it?"

"Yeah, sis," Ashlyn jumps in. "What's your plan?"

"I believe you are confused. There is no plan. Beckett doesn't want me. He thinks I'm incompetent and that I can't meet my deadlines."

I can't help it – a snarl spills out at the end. How dare he think I'm incapable of meeting my deadlines? My personnel file clearly shows how capable I am.

"Has he told you he thinks you're incompetent?" Ashlyn asks.

"He questions my work constantly. Makes me report to him in person rather than via email as I did with his predecessor. He doesn't believe I can meet my deadlines."

"Huh. I assumed literal Lilac wouldn't make assumptions about a person's thoughts."

I glare at Aspen. "I'm not making assumptions. I'm drawing conclusions from his actions."

She rubs her hands together. "This is going to be fun."

What is she referring to? "What is going to be fun?"

"You'll see," she sings.

Aspen can't possibly believe Beckett questioning my work and my work ethic is an indicator of his sexual interest in me. She's obviously been reading too many of those romance books she stocks in abundance at her bookstore, *Fall Into A Good Book*.

She stands. "Who's ready for karaoke at the bar?"

"I can't. I have deadlines." And karaoke is one of my least favorite activities. I can't carry a tune and prefer to perform activities I'm competent at.

She rolls her eyes. "Naturally, you do."

I expect my sisters to cajole me into joining them at *Electric Vibes,* the only bar in town, but they follow Aspen out of my apartment without a single word.

I trail after them to the door and shut it while contemplating what they've said. Are they correct? Is Beckett acting this way due to some kind of sexual tension between us? I know I'm sexually attracted to him, but is he sexually attracted to me as well?

No. It's highly improbable. I shouldn't let my sisters put thoughts into my mind. Especially when all of them are obsessed with sex and having babies. I'm happy they're happy, but a relationship is not in my future. It's not the path I've chosen. My career is my future.

Chapter 5

Inappropriate – committing an act you really, really want to but know you shouldn't

BECKETT

I listen to the phone ring through the speakers of my car and scowl when my call remains unanswered. Lilac is once again ignoring me. Since it's two o'clock in the afternoon on a weekday, she can't claim I'm blurring the line between work and personal.

Unless she's in a hotel with some man somewhere. I hear the leather on the steering wheel crack and realize I'm squeezing the life out of it. *Shit.* I loosen my grip as I remind myself what Lilac does in her private time with other men is not my business.

Yes, Lilac is a gorgeous woman I'd enjoy the hell out of getting to know better, but she's also my employee. I can't go there.

I touch the disconnect button on my display. There's really no reason to phone Lilac since I'll be seeing her in a few minutes at the site for the biomass project outside of Winter Falls anyway.

The biomass project is Lilac's brainchild. The small power plant will burn cornstalks from the farms around the area to produce steam to run a turbine, which will provide heat for the homes in Winter Falls.

Biomass is controversial as clean energy due to the pollution created from burning natural materials, but Lilac has developed a method to limit the pollution and associated smell. Her ideas are revolutionary.

I pull into the construction site and park in front of a trailer next to Lilac's car. When I exit my car, I search the area for Lilac. I catch sight of brown, silky hair under a construction hat, and my legs automatically carry me in her direction.

"Uh oh, someone's PMSing," a man grumbles as I reach them.

I step forward to interfere, but Lilac speaks before I have the chance. "Would you say a man is PMSing when he points out a mistake you've made?"

"Well—"

"No, you wouldn't. Because he's a man."

"And, therefore, can't have PMS."

Someone's being obstinate. I lean back against a partially finished wall and cross my legs at the ankle to settle in for the show.

"You're missing the point. On purpose, I might add."

He lifts his hard hat to scratch his hair. "And the point is?"

Lilac crosses her arms over her chest and glares at him. "It's inappropriate to claim a woman is on her menstrual cycle because she's brusque or aggressive."

The man holds up his hands. "I didn't mean to offend."

"No, you meant to belittle me."

"Hey now, I didn't mean anything by the comment."

"Maybe your conscious brain *thinks* you didn't mean anything by the comment, although I'm not convinced. Why else would you use the term 'PMSing' in a work environment? But your subconscious brain definitely has a hidden agenda. It's known as unconscious bias for a reason."

I don't know what it says about me but listening to Lilac school a man half a foot taller than her and at least fifty pounds heavier is one of the sexiest things I've ever seen.

"Why don't I apologize, and we put this whole incident behind us?" the man suggests.

Not a bad idea, but I know Lilac won't go for it. She's sunk her teeth into the altercation now.

"I accept your apology, but we won't put this whole incident behind us, because the next woman you speak those words to may be cowed by them and I can't accept such a possibility. I'm recommending you attend an unconscious bias training."

The man's neck darkens and his teeth clench. "Fine," he mutters before marching off.

"And I expect you to make the changes I suggested as well," Lilac hollers after him.

She makes a note on her tablet before slamming it shut. "What do you want?"

I scan the area. Is she talking to me?

"Yes, I'm talking to you."

I step forward. "I didn't realize you knew I was here."

She pivots to face me. "Of course, I knew you were there. I'm a woman. I learned early on in life I need to be aware of my surroundings at all times."

I growl. "Has someone hurt you? Who is he? Where is he?"

She waves away my concern. "I'm perfectly capable of handling myself."

I notice she didn't answer my question. I open my mouth to repeat my questions but realize – no matter how much I may wish otherwise – it's technically none of my business. Unless she was harassed on the job.

"Has anyone sexually harassed you while you've been working for us?"

"No. And, if they had, you could have read about it in my personnel file as all harassment incidents are documented by HR."

I roll my shoulders and decide to let this go. Lilac is not *mine* to take care of. She will never be mine to take care of. Even if she weren't my employee, she wouldn't be mine. Not considering the smorgasbord of men at her disposal. My hands fist at the thought.

"The macho man business is handled. Now, can you please answer my question as to why you are here?"

I shrug. "I came to check on the site."

Her eyes narrow. "You came to check on the site on the day you knew I was here?"

I could lie and say it's a coincidence, but I'd probably get a lecture about how coincidences aren't real due to some subconscious thought. The woman has an opinion on everything, which is her prerogative, but she also has entirely too much knowledge on a variety of subjects. I'll never win an argument with her.

"I wanted to observe your interaction with the local crew."

She flinches. "And caught me reprimanding the foreman."

"I…"

She squares her shoulders and speaks before I figure out what to say. "I will not tolerate men and their prejudice against women on the job site. I won't hesitate to call someone out for their conduct if it is inappropriate. I have no plans to change my behavior in this regard. If you have an issue with it, I suggest you discuss it with HR."

The woman is a goddess with her back held straight, her chin jutted out, and her eyes on fire. I want to fist her hair and claim her mouth – to hell with the consequences – but she'd probably knee me in the balls before verballing ripping me a new asshole.

I growl. "I don't believe women should accept inappropriate male behavior."

"Good. At least, we agree in this area. Now, if there isn't anything else?"

She begins marching off before I have a chance to answer her question.

"But we do need to discuss one thing," I holler after her.

"Which is?" She asks without turning around.

"Your inability to answer the phone—"

She twirls around and stomps toward me. "I have told you I am under no obligation to answer my phone during my personal time. If you continue to insist I do, I will notify HR."

"I'm not referring to out of office hours. I tried reaching you before I arrived on site."

She digs her phone out of her pocket and wakens the screen. "You called at five minutes past two. I was in a meeting from one o'clock until two-fifteen."

"Then, you did hear your phone?"

"No. My phone is on silent during meetings. It's rude to answer your phone during a meeting."

"It's rude to ignore your boss."

"I wasn't ignoring you. It's impossible to ignore someone if you don't realize they're trying to reach you."

I grunt. "You don't have to interpret everything someone says literally all the time."

"Why not? What other interpretation should I have made?"

"I assumed you were avoiding my calls since you've done so on numerous occasions in the past and it's not appropriate."

"I thought we settled this matter." Her nose wrinkles as she considers my words. "Wait. Is this why you came to the job site today? You weren't observing my interactions with the crew. You were checking up on me, because you don't trust me."

"I trust you."

She cocks an eyebrow. "You do? Your trust is why you attempt to contact me at all times of the day and night to discuss my work?"

"It's not all times of the day and night."

"I don't understand what I've done to make you think I'm not competent to handle my job. I finish my projects on time and often under budget. I'm the first one in the office every day and often the last one to leave. Perhaps we need to have a sit down with HR and discuss how to address this situation." She nods as if coming to a conclusion. "I'll make an appointment when I'm back in the office."

She starts to leave, but I grab her bicep to stop her. She stares down at my hand on her bicep.

Shit. I shouldn't have touched her. It's inappropriate but damned if I want to release her. She's wearing a thin blouse and I can feel the heat of her body through the material. My thumb moves without my meaning it to and rubs circles in her underarm. Goosebumps break out on her skin before she yanks her arm away.

"I will see you back at the office," she gasps out, proving she's as affected by me as I am by her.

"Drive safe."

"I'm an excellent driver," she says before whirling on her heel and stomping away.

If I were a better man, I'd say I didn't watch her ass bounce as she leaves. Apparently, I'm not a better man as my eyes are glued to her backside. My hands itch to mold those perfect cheeks in my hands.

I pull at my collar as my neck warms. Talk about inappropriate.

Chapter 6

Bet – a passive aggressive way to let someone know how you feel without actually telling them

"You owe me five bucks," Ashlyn says and holds out her hand to Juniper as I enter the town hall for the monthly business meeting.

"What are you talking about? I never bet you five bucks."

One of the favorite pastimes in Winter Falls is gambling. The residents will bet on everything. Personally, I believe betting is a dangerous habit, but when I suggested banning the practice, I was nearly kicked out of town. I'm serious. They took a vote, and I barely survived.

"Yeah, you did. You said Lilac was too chicken to show up at this month's town hall meeting."

Juniper snorts. "I would never. Lilac has a strong sense of community. I knew she would show up. A typical middle child really."

"Actually, a middle child usually has less of a sense of belonging," I point out. "Although I do not subscribe to pseudo-psychology claiming birth order has an effect on personality development."

If I used words such as hogwash – which I don't – I would refer to the whole 'middle-child syndrome' as hogwash. I refuse to believe being the third child in a family of five affected my growth.

"Also, did you forget you're a middle child, too, Juniper?"

There are five of us and since Aspen is the oldest and Ashlyn the youngest, there are three middle children. Ellery, myself, and Juniper – in that order.

"But you're right smack dab in the middle," Juniper contests.

"And yet we loved our baby girls equally," Mom says as she arrives and plants a kiss on my cheek. She winks at me, too, but I'm not clear as to why. Is it a secret she loves all of her children? She's not doing a very good job of hiding her secret in that event.

"Except I gave you a grandchild first, so I'm currently your favorite," Ellery says as she arrives with her fiancé Cole and their baby Willow.

"Give me," Mom says but doesn't wait for Ellery to comply before stealing her grandchild away from her.

"I may not have given Mom a grandchild," Aspen says and pain flashes in her eyes. I file away the information for later. "But I'm the oldest, which means I'm the favorite."

"Please, I'm the favorite because I'm the youngest. They stopped making children after I came along because they had found perfection," Ashlyn claims.

"Or we were too tired to have sex with five small children running around," Mom claims.

Ashlyn feigns gagging. "Ugh. Stop. No talk about your sex life. Especially not in front of the baby."

"You brought it up." Mom shrugs. "Besides, I'm fairly certain Willow doesn't understand what we're talking about."

Ashlyn ignores Mom, "Anyway, I'm having a baby and giving Mom a grandchild, too. I definitely win this round."

Her husband, Rowan, arrives and throws his arm around her shoulders before kissing her hair. "Life's not a contest, Dream girl."

"Yes, it is. And I'm winning."

I'm not sure how life as a contest would work. Do you win because you have the most money? The most children? You die old? Life cannot be a contest. The parameters are undefined.

"What are we talking about?" Lyric asks and interrupts my musings about how contests should be properly defined.

I point to Ellery. "She thinks she's the favorite because she was the first daughter to give Mom a grandchild." I point to Ashlyn. "She thinks she's the favorite because she's the youngest and pregnant." I point to Juniper. "She's being quiet because she's missing Maverick."

"The house feels empty without him," Juniper mumbles.

"And Aspen—"

Aspen coughs. "He didn't ask for a play-by-play."

He asked what we were talking about. I'm not sure how my answer is wrong. I study my oldest sister and the way her fiancé is cuddling her. She has black smudges under her eyes indicating she hasn't been sleeping well. She's also being quieter than usual.

Based on the above indications, she's sad. But why? Is it because she hasn't conceived yet? Do I ask her? No, she cut me off. She obviously doesn't want to discuss the situation in front of everyone. Should I phone her later?

Although, everyone knows I'm not the best person to deal with feelings. It's not as if I don't understand feelings like my sisters claim. I just don't know how to communicate my sympathy in a way they approve of.

The alarm on Ashlyn's phone goes off, and I check the clock on the wall. It's time to begin the meeting. I follow Ashlyn as she skips to the front of the room.

Ashlyn is currently the mayor of Winter Falls. She wasn't elected. The townspeople don't believe in electing a mayor. Instead, every year we choose a business owner from a hat to lead us through the next year. Yes, a hat. If I didn't assist in the 'choosing', I wouldn't believe it either.

Personally, I think the position should be a paid one. Candidates should submit applications and undergo a rigorous hiring procedure. But when I suggested as much to Dad, who is the town's lawyer, he laughed. I don't know why and when I asked him why he just laughed harder. And everyone thinks I'm the confusing one.

Bang! Bang! Bang!

I inhale a deep breath before I wrestle the gavel out of Ashlyn's hands. Don't misunderstand me. A gavel is a perfectly appropriate item for the mayor to wield, but there's no reason to hit it against a table with such vigor it leaves dents.

After she brings the meeting to order, she states, "We'll begin with an update of the community center project by Cole."

Cole kisses Ellery's cheek before standing. He's the architect and project manager for the community center the town is currently building. As a matter of fact, the two of them met when he came to town to pitch his firm for the project and stayed at her establishment, *The Inn on Main*.

They had a one-night stand and Ellery ended up pregnant. Initially, she wanted nothing to do with Cole, but he managed to change her mind in the end.

"I don't have much to report since our previous monthly meeting," he begins before filling us in on the current situation.

Once he finishes, he motions for me to continue. I'm the comptroller of Winter Falls, and as such, it's my duty to ensure the project stays on budget. Being on budget is no longer an issue, however, as Ashlyn and Juniper came into a windfall worth half a million dollars. The story of how they solved a decades old mystery would be preposterous, except it's true.

"Regarding the expenditures—"

"We want an update on the biomass project," Sage interrupts to demand from the back of the room.

"Yeah, Lilac, how's the project going?" Feather asks from next to Sage.

Sage and Feather are part of what the town refers to as the gossip gals. Together with Petal, Cayenne, and Clove, the ladies believe it is their duty in life to ferret out all the secrets in Winter Falls. I've explained to them the definition of privacy over a hundred times, but they refuse to listen.

In addition to aspiring to be the biggest gossips in the world, they fancy themselves matchmakers and are convinced they're responsible for my four sisters being in love. Personally, I believe they hindered more than helped, but I've learned to keep my opinions to myself when it comes to the five elderly ladies.

I clear my throat. "As you know, the biomass power plant will provide energy to heat the homes in Winter Falls."

"Boring!" Petal shouts. "We want all the news on you and the dreamy Beckett."

"Yeah," Clove yells her agreement. "Rumor has it the two of you were hot and heavy at the construction site."

"I heard a man harassed her and her hunk of a boss, Beckett, came and saved her," Sage claims.

How ridiculous! I've never needed saving from a man. I'm perfectly capable of taking care of myself. Are they fabricating rumors?

"Beckett did not save me, and no one harassed me."

Instead of responding to the truth of my statement and stopping the false rumors, Sage removes a large notebook from her bag and opens it. "I'm accepting dates starting from tomorrow."

I contemplate how to handle this situation. Obviously, Sage has decided to make my relationship with Beckett into some type of bet. I could argue with her, but I've never won an argument with her before. Mostly because she claims she's correct and leaves while you're in the middle of explaining your point of view to her.

Bang! Bang! Bang!

Ashlyn's holding up the gavel as if she's ready to use it hit someone.

"No getting into fist fights when you're pregnant," Mom hollers across the room.

"You're not supposed to tell anyone I'm pregnant. And, I prefer the term knocked up."

"If you didn't want anyone to know you're pregnant, you shouldn't have bought pregnancy tests at *Nature Coop*."

"Beginner mistake." Ellery snorts. "You always go out of town for pregnancy tests and condoms."

"Why would you go out of town for condoms?" Mom asks. "You know I have everyone in town covered with regard to prophylactics."

This is true. My mother is on a mission to ensure the entire world practices safe sex.

"Do you want me to knock on your door at 3 a.m.?" Ellery asks and Cole groans.

Mom's brow wrinkles. "Why would you knock? You know the door isn't locked and you know where I keep my stock-pile."

Every West daughter knows where Mom keeps her supply of condoms since she began showing us where it was before we were teenagers. While my sisters are embarrassed whenever Mom mentions condoms to them, I appreciate our mother's pragmatism.

Bang! Bang! Bang!

"Can you stop talking about your sex life now?" Ashlyn asks Mom.

"She wasn't talking about her sex life," I point out. "And why does this freak you out? You're pregnant. Everyone knows you've had sex, but we're not pretending to gag like we're teenagers."

"You… you …you…"

While Ashlyn searches for words, I decide it's time to finish this meeting before the chaos takes over. I have more work I want to finish after this since my boss still believes I'm incompetent. I don't know why I'm trying to prove my worth to him. Everyone else in the company is aware of how dedicated and hardworking I am.

I consult the agenda and realize the only remaining item is the Litha festival. Since I'm the chairperson of the festival committee and we have a meeting scheduled for later this week, I decide we can skip the item.

"This meeting is adjourned," I announce.

I watch to ensure the town secretary, River, makes a note of the end of the meeting. River is Lyric's brother and does all kinds of odd jobs for the town. He's a part-time volunteer firefighter, a deputy when needed, and the note taker at these meetings.

I gather my things and proceed toward the exit.

"You can't go," Sage hollers at me from across the room.

"Of course, I can."

"But—"

"Have a lovely evening," I shout over whatever plea she was planning on making.

I know better than to allow myself to be cornered by Sage or any of the other gossip gals. They believe it's their duty as gossipmongers to interrogate you until they learn all of your secrets.

Normally, I don't mind their interference. After all, I usually don't have any secrets. Or, at least, no secrets about my private life. They're not interested in my work secrets.

But not now. Beckett isn't exactly a secret, but the way my body yearns for him is. It's not a yearning I plan to act on, but it is a yearning I don't need anyone else knowing about. Especially not the five women who have their sights on matchmaking me.

I scurry out of the room. I've studied history. I know when a retreat is my best option.

Chapter 7

Mixed messages – a showing of feelings diametrically opposed to each other causing people to think you have a personality disorder

MY LIPS PURSE AS I stare at the aisle of products encased in plastic. Doing groceries at this store in White Bridge does not have my preference considering its lack of environmental consciousness, but the only store in Winter Falls, *Nature Coop,* closes at 8 p.m.

I consult my watch. It's 7:15. I do have enough time to drive to *Nature Coop* and buy the few items I need for dinner and breakfast tomorrow, but I'm planning to return to the office. Driving back and forth to Winter Falls would be a waste of energy no matter how efficient my mini electric car is.

There must be something I can buy to eat that isn't un-necessarily wrapped in plastic. Maybe fruit. As I'm examining the strawberries and melons, a woman hollers my name. I turn around to discover Cassandra rushing toward me with her arms open wide.

"Lilac! Lilac!" She continues to shout even though I'm staring directly at her.

I place my basket in front of me before she can hug me. I saw Beckett's eldest sister a few days ago. There's no reason to greet me with a hug. I haven't been away for months on a scientific mission to the Antarctic.

Her hands drop and she skids to a halt in front of me. "I didn't expect to see you here."

My lips purse of their own accord. "I do not prefer to do my shopping here."

She laughs. "I should have known. Beckett's the same. He gets one of those farm delivery boxes every week, so he can avoid this 'shrine to plastic'."

He does? I didn't realize Beckett had an environmental conscious. Despite being the CEO of an environmental engineering business, he isn't an environmental engineer. The man was hired because of his business acumen, not his environmental knowledge.

Silence falls and I have no idea how to fill it, so I decide to extract myself from the situation. "I need to be going. I want to return to work."

Cassandra moves to block me. "Nuh-uh. No way. You aren't going back to work. You're coming to dinner with me."

"I have a project I need to finish."

"It can wait until after you've eaten. Isn't eating good for the brain or something?"

"It is true a drop of blood glucose levels does have an affect on concentration."

She removes the basket from my hands and places it on the ground. "It's settled then. You're coming to dinner with me."

I motion toward her empty hands. "Where are your groceries?"

"Oh, I didn't come in here to buy anything. I saw your car parked in the lot and followed you inside."

"I thought you said you didn't expect to see me here, and how do you know what my car looks like anyway?"

She snorts. "Not many people drive a tiny electric car in this region."

She is not incorrect. Entirely too many people in the region outside of Winter Falls enjoy driving in SUVs, although I've yet to puzzle out what sport they're utilizing the vehicles for.

We exit the store, and I consider the row of restaurants. "Where shall we go?"

She threads her arm through mine. "Don't be silly. There's only one environmentally conscious restaurant in town you approve of, and you need a reservation. We'll go to my house."

"How do you know there's only one restaurant in town I approve of?" Because she is correct. White Bridge only has one restaurant I eat at.

"Duh. Because Beckett will only eat at one restaurant."

Another surprise about my boss. I don't enjoy being surprised, despite this being a pleasant one. I prefer to have all the facts and figures at my disposal. How did I not realize Beckett is as environmentally conscious as I am? Are there other aspects of the man I've misunderstood?

I follow Cassandra to her house. When we arrive, I note there are several cars in the driveway. All are electric cars, although not the economical brand I drive.

Before I can exit my vehicle, she's there opening it for me and hauling me out. "Come on. Dinner should be ready by now."

"Ready by now? Don't you need to cook it? And who do all these cars belong to?"

She hums but doesn't answer my questions.

"We're here," she greets as we walk into the house.

"Here? Isn't this your house?"

"Finally! We were about to start without you," Beckett responds.

Beckett? Why is he here? I halt in the entryway. Cassandra rolls her eyes before tightening her grasp on me and dragging me further into the house.

"Guess who I found inspecting the strawberries at the store."

Beckett's smile freezes on his face. "Cassandra," he growls.

"What? I couldn't allow her to buy fruit at the plastic emporium, now could I?"

"It's fine. I didn't realize you were here. Cassandra said we were eating at her house. She didn't mention we wouldn't be eating alone."

I yank my hand out of her grip and whirl around to march to the door. But when I open it, a hand slams it shut again.

I glance over my shoulder at Beckett. "What are you doing?"

"You don't have to leave."

"Of course, I do. You're having some sort of family dinner. I'm not family."

"Anyone who puts up with grumpy face as much as you do is family," Cassandra says from where she's standing behind

Beckett. Elizabeth and Gabrielle join her and nod in agreement.

"A face can't be grumpy."

Beckett grins down at me and his blue eyes sparkle. This close to him I notice there are specks of gray in his blue irises. The slight imperfection only serves to make his face even more handsome. Dang him. His expression is anything but bad-tempered and I feel the corners of my lips tug up.

"There she is," he whispers.

"Who? Did you forget who I am? I'm Lilac West. I work for you as an environmental engineer at *Clean Mountain Environment*. Are you having memory problems? Should we schedule an MRI for you?"

He barks out a laugh and drops the hand blocking me. "Come on." He indicates the interior of the house. "Let's get you fed."

My stomach rumbles at the mention of food. I ignore it. "I'm serious. If you're having memory problems, they should be medically investigated."

He grasps my hand and leads me to the dining room. My hand tingles at the feel of his skin on mine. The tingle travels through my body until it reaches my core. With a start, I realize I'm sexually aroused by a single touch from Beckett.

I wrench my hand from his. He's my boss. It's inappropriate to have any type of sexual feeling for him.

He holds out a chair for me and I manage to accept his gesture without touching him. Unfortunately, the gentleman act has as much an effect on my body as him touching me. I shouldn't be here. I should go.

Beckett pushes the chair in and leans down to whisper in my ear. "Eat your dinner, Lilac."

His breath caresses my skin, which does not help my body to calm down. In fact, my body is burning up. I duck my head and reach for my glass of water. By the time I've finished the entire glass, I feel more in control of my body.

"I hope you eat eggplant," Cassandra says as she sets a dish on the table. "Because Gabrielle made a ton of eggplant lasagna."

Gabrielle blushes and tucks her chin into her chest.

"I love eggplant lasagna."

"You're not a vegan, are you?" Elizabeth asks.

Beckett barks out a laugh.

"Why are you laughing? What's funny about me being a vegan?"

I'm not a vegan, but I do usually stick to goat cheese and milk from Lyric's brother's farm. I know Phoenix and trust him not to abuse the environment.

"Because I've seen you inhale cheese."

My brow furrows. "Inhale cheese? You can't inhale cheese. Well, I guess you could if you ground it up into powder, but then you'd miss the enjoyment of the flavor on your tongue. Not to mention texture is an important aspect of flavor as well."

"I wasn't being literal."

Oh. I'm not oblivious to figurative interpretations of phrases and words, but I do sometimes forget about them in the heat of the moment. There is a reason my sisters refer to me as Literal

Lilac after all. They think I don't know, but I do. I try not to let their joking upset me. I know they love me and would never intentionally hurt my feelings.

I bite into the lasagna and moan as the flavor of spicy marinara sauce and ricotta cheese combined with grilled eggplant hits my tongue. I savor it as I chew.

"This is fabulous," I tell Gabrielle. "It's better than my mom's but don't tell her. She can be prickly when you don't enjoy her food."

Gabrielle beams at me. "You really think it tastes good?"

"Of course. I don't lie."

Beckett clears his throat. When I glance his way, he mouths *thank you* to me. I don't know why he's thanking me. The man is confusing. He's angry with me ninety-one percent of the time at work – and, yes, I did the math – but he wanted me to stay when I arrived at his sister's house this evening.

I don't enjoy mixed messages and I abhor the games men and women play. I don't know what game Beckett thinks he's playing with me, but I refuse to be a participant. He confuses me and I do not enjoy being confused.

Chapter 8

Whiplash – when your head spins due to your boss acting hot and then cold toward you for no apparent reason

BECKETT STICKS HIS HEAD into my office and scowls at me before asking, "Are you ready for the meeting?"

Why is he scowling at me? Last night he was all smiles and compliments. Is he constipated? Too much cheese can cause constipation after all.

I open my mouth to ask him but, according to Aspen, defecation should not be discussed in a work environment. When I was filling in for her at her bookstore, I asked a customer who was taking an over average amount of time in the restroom if she was constipated.

Apparently, those types of questions are embarrassing and are best left unspoken. I'm still uncertain as to why. Human biology is an essential part of life.

"Of course, I'm ready. Why wouldn't I be ready? This meeting has been on the calendar for a month now," I say instead of mentioning his possible intestinal problems.

"The city of Arkville would be our largest client yet."

Why is he telling me information of which I'm already aware? "I know."

"I want to nail this presentation."

He wants to nail this presentation? I'm the one giving the presentation, not him.

"Are you going to stand there and tell me things I already know all morning, or are you going to let me work?"

He grunts and exits my office without speaking another word.

I thought after last night he would stop questioning my work. He was perfectly pleasant as he joked with his sisters at dinner. I guess I misunderstood. It's not the first time I've misunderstood a social situation. Based on my statistical analysis, it won't be the last.

Or, I need to revisit the constipation hypothesis. But since I can't confirm or deny whether he is constipated, the hypothesis is at a dead end.

I check the time and adjust my billing for the five minutes of work time Beckett wasted. I'll add those five minutes to the hundreds of hours I've wasted since he took over the position of CEO at the company. I wish I was exaggerating, but I don't exaggerate. Exaggerating is akin to lying and I avoid it at all costs.

When my alarm buzzes to indicate the meeting with Arkville is set to begin in five minutes, I stand and shrug on my blazer before gathering my things and making my way to the conference room.

The conference room is already buzzing when I arrive. Because of the scale of the project, there are several engineers attending the meeting as well as Beckett and Norman, the CFO.

Beckett glares at me before pointing to the chair next to his, but I ignore him and sit beside another engineer. I wish I could lie and say I chose this seat because I'll be working with this engineer should we procure this project, but the truth is my body is entirely too attuned to Beckett's.

Sitting next to him during a meeting will be distracting, and I don't allow anything to distract me from my work. I haven't yet figured out how to shut off my body's response to his, but I will. I can accomplish anything I set my mind to.

Beckett's nostrils flare as he once again points to the chair next to him. What is his problem now? Why is he mad at me this time? The man is confusing, and I prefer to stay away from confusing situations. I always end up making a fool of myself in them. I return my attention to my tablet.

Jack, the engineer on my left, elbows me. "I think the boss is trying to get your attention."

I make some non-committal sound as I continue to peruse the presentation. There's no need to re-read it as I have it memorized, but anything is better than dealing with Beckett and the confusing signals he sends me.

"His face is getting red."

I peek over at Beckett from beneath my lashes. His teeth are clenched, and his hands are fisted. He snaps his fingers at me before motioning to the chair next to him.

"You better sit next to him before he has a heart attack."

I wish I could indulge in a fantasy of him having a heart attack for a few moments, but I don't indulge in fantasies. I leave those to my sisters. Besides, I'm from Winter Falls where non-violence is preached from the moment of birth. I'm fairly certain wishing injury on someone is considered wrong in their view.

I gather my things and relocate to the seat he indicated.

"Are you done flirting with Jack?" Beckett asks through clenched teeth as I settle in my seat.

I want to remind him who I flirt with is none of his business as it falls under the 'personal' and not 'work' flag, but I notice a few people glancing in our direction. Despite being in the right, I know it's better to not correct the boss in front of other people.

It's one of those things I don't understand about personal communication. Why is it wrong to correct someone in front of others? I don't get offended when someone corrects me. Although, it rarely happens as I don't make many mistakes. But after receiving several reprimands from HR on the matter, I decided it was safer to follow their advice in this regard.

"What are you talking about? Jack is married and has three boys. Did you forget? I think you should seriously consider scheduling the MRI we discussed last night."

"Last night?" Norman leans forward to catch my gaze. "What do you mean last night? Were you working late?"

Before I can tell him I was working late – I returned to the office after dinner after all – Beckett answers, "We had dinner together last night."

At his announcement, everyone in the room ceases speaking and swivels their head to stare in our direction.

"I had dinner with his sister Cassandra last night. I didn't know Beckett would join us."

My words aren't exactly a lie. I did have dinner with Cassandra and Beckett did join us. Although, my boss joined us prior to the commencement of the meal, and I could have left before eating dinner with him. Obviously, I should have left upon seeing him. I did try but not hard enough.

Beckett snorts. "Since dinner was a family affair, it wasn't much of a stretch for me to join you."

I glare at him. What is he doing? Does he want everyone in the company to think we're involved? Being involved is against company policy. I would lose my job.

Is this his plan? To have me fired? Granted, it would be easier to have me fired for personal misconduct than my work being subpar since my work is never subpar. I need to consider this angle further, but not when I'm about to give the most important presentation of my career.

"I didn't realize Cassandra invited me to a family meal. I apologize for any inconvenience caused."

"Perhaps the two of you could discuss your dinner plans when we're not about to meet with an important client," Norman suggests in a tone signaling it's not a suggestion.

The client arrives and everyone stands to introduce themselves. Once the introductions are finished, Beckett signals for me to begin.

"Ms. West will lead us through a presentation of how *Clean Mountain Environment* can assist Arkville in the planning and designing of facilities to handle its municipal waste."

I stand and indicate the screen where my PowerPoint presentation is now showing. The lights dim and I begin.

"Let me explain what *Clean Mountain Environment* is and how we can help you," I start.

As I speak, I can feel all the eyes in the room centered on me. I'm used to giving presentations and usually don't notice the attention. I don't normally experience nervousness in a work environment, but this time doesn't feel normal.

I scan the room to figure out why. My gaze lands on Beckett. He doesn't bother to shift his gaze away from me. He continues to stare at me with obvious heat in his eyes.

A thrill runs through my body at the feel of his eyes upon me, and I trip on the carpet and tumble toward the floor. Jack catches me before I can fall.

"You okay?" he asks with his hand firmly gripping my elbow to steady me.

Someone growls, and my head whips to the side to discover Beckett's gaze is now focused on Jack's hand. I wrench my arm free.

"I'm fine."

I manage to finish my presentation without any further incident. I sink into my seat next to Beckett and inhale a few deep breaths to calm my racing heart. I can't believe I nearly ruined the presentation. After everything I said to him about being prepared, I nearly wrecked our chances to procure Arkville as a client.

Beckett's hand lands on my thigh and he squeezes.

"Good job."

What? Why is he complimenting me now when I screwed up? Did he miss my tripping? No, I know he didn't. He wouldn't have been annoyed by Jack touching my elbow if he had.

And why was he annoyed anyway? If I had ended up sprawled on the floor, it would have been a disaster.

I'm beginning to understand what Ashlyn said about the mixed signals she received from Rowan before they were married. Perhaps I need to discuss my problems with Beckett with her. The idea doesn't fill me with joy as my sister will use the conversation as an excuse to invade my private life.

The situation with my boss cannot continue as it is, however, and I will not quit my job, which is the simplest solution. As I'm in need of advice, I may be forced to allow my family into my personal life. I do not relish the prospect.

Chapter 9

Misunderstand – incorrectly interpret a situation causing you to act like an ass

BECKETT

I enter Lilac's office and scowl when I notice she's packing up for the evening.

"Arkville asked several questions about your presentation from the other day. I need you to stay late to answer them."

She pauses with her packing to glower at me. "Those questions were emailed to us less than an hour ago. Surely, they can wait until tomorrow."

Her phone buzzes in her hand and she glimpses down at it. She rolls her eyes at whatever's written there but her lips tip up in a smile as she types out a quick response. Is she seriously messaging with one of her lovers while I'm standing right here in front of her?

"Are you too busy for work?" I grit out.

She startles and nearly drops her phone. Gotcha! I cough to hide my amusement.

She quickly recovers to glare at me. "It's after seven. Everyone else left the office before six. I think it's fair to say I've been busy with work."

"Since you're already here, you won't mind staying to get these questions answered."

I'm an asshole. I overheard her talking to Jack about needing to quit work on time today as she has plans for tonight. As soon as the email from the city of Arkville arrived, I knew fate was on my side. She's not joining any man on some date tonight. Not if I can help it.

"I'll answer them at home later. I have an appointment now."

I snap my mouth shut before I can growl at her and her 'appointment'. I don't have any business growling at an employee, but Lilac gets under my skin in a way no one before her has.

"I prefer to go over your answers with you," I say instead of admitting I'm a jealous bastard who doesn't want her going out on any dates with another man despite knowing we can't be together.

"Okay," she agrees despite my trampling all over her independent work ethic. "I'll write up my answers tonight and send them to you. We can go over them in the morning before I respond to Arkville."

"I can't do the morning."

I'm a fucking liar. I have no plans in the morning except to work out before arriving at the office. Now, I'll have to make up an appointment, or else she'll figure out what a liar I am.

She fists her hands at her hips. "And I can't do the evening."

"We're at a Mexican standoff."

"No, we're not," she denies. "A Mexican standoff suggests no party can achieve victory. There's an easy solution here."

I cock an eyebrow and lean against her doorway as if I've got all night to listen to her lecture me on Mexican standoffs. "Which is?"

"Easy. I send you my responses, you read through them when you have the time, and we meet sometime tomorrow to discuss them."

It is an easy solution. But it's unacceptable as it ends with her being able to go on her date tonight.

Her phone beeps again and this time she giggles when she reads the message. I've never heard Lilac giggle before and now she's giggling for some other man. I shove my hands in my pockets before she notices they're fisted.

"I have a full day tomorrow." At the rate my lies are piling up, I'll never dig my way out of this.

"As do I, but I can make fifteen minutes available for you. If you do the same, we have a perfectly acceptable solution."

"No," I growl.

"No? Are you constipated again?"

I bark out a laugh. "Excuse me?"

"Never mind," she mutters. "Forget I asked."

"No. I want to discuss this."

Her head tilts to the side as she studies me. "You do? My sisters said I'm not allowed to discuss defecation at the office."

I chuckle. "Defecation?"

"It is the proper terminology."

"It's also a word adults don't use except for scientists and doctors."

Her cheeks darken, but her voice is steady when she responds, "I'm a scientist."

"I wouldn't refer to an engineer as a scientist."

She clears her throat. "A scientist is a person who studies or has expert knowledge of one or more of the natural or physical sciences. In addition to my engineering degree, I have a master's degree in biology, which I believe qualifies me as a scientist in this regard."

This is an absurd discussion. Why are we talking about the definition of a scientist? Oh right. Because I'm the asshole who embarrassed her when I found her use of the word defecation amusing.

"Anyway, I'm not constipated."

"Good. Constipation is a symptom of colon cancer. I would hate for you to be ill."

I stand up straight. "You would?"

Her brow wrinkles. "Yes, I would. I do not wish harm on anyone," she claims, but she won't meet my gaze.

Lilac is a straight shooter. She never lies, but she's being evasive now and I want to know about what. Before I have a chance to ask, her phone beeps again.

She reads the message before picking up her briefcase. "I really do need to leave now."

Not on my watch. "You are not running off on some date while we have work to do."

"What are you talking about?"

"I was speaking English, wasn't I?"

"Of course, you were speaking English – according to your personnel file, you don't speak any foreign languages – but your words made no sense."

I forgot I need to be literal with Lilac. She doesn't understand innuendos or ambiguities.

"We have work to do. Your date can be postponed or, better yet, cancelled."

"You're speaking English, but your words are still confusing. What makes you think I have a date?"

I wave toward her phone. "You laughing and giggling while reading messages from some man while I'm standing here in front of you."

"I don't giggle," she protests.

"Whatever. You laughing then."

"Hold on. You're upset because you think I have a date this evening?"

"I know you do. I heard you tell Jack all about it."

She snorts. "Obviously, you didn't listen to everything I told Jack because then you would know tonight's date is with my sisters."

Relief slams into me with such a force, I grasp the doorknob to stop myself from rushing to her. "Your sisters?"

"Yes, I have four of them."

I know she does as I met three of them, but she never shares private information with me. I'm not letting this opportunity pass me by. "Where are you in the mix?"

She sighs. "Please tell me you don't ascribe to the pseu-do-psychology concerning birth order."

I grin. "One of the middle children, then?"

She narrows her eyes on me. "How did you know?"

"The oldest and the youngest child always insist on telling everyone where they are in the birth order," I explain.

"Huh. I didn't realize this. I'll have to observe my family closer to ascertain if your hypothesis is correct," she says before making a note in her phone to do just that. "Now, if you'll excuse me, I need to depart. I'm already late as it is."

I shrug. "You can be a few minutes late for dinner."

"We're not having dinner. Tonight is book club."

"Book club?"

"Yes, I can read, you know." She huffs. "And they picked out a book especially for me. Although why a grumpy boss romance with an enemies to lovers theme is for me, I'll never understand."

"Your sisters chose a grumpy boss romance for you to read?"

"Are you having auditory perception problems now? Maybe you should have a full physical work up in addition to the MRI."

"I'm not having auditory perception problems." But I may be having heart problems since her sisters choosing a grumpy boss romance for her to read means they're on my side. Maybe being with Lilac isn't a lost cause after all.

I step forward into the room and shut the door behind me.

"What are you doing? I literally just told you I need to leave. You can't keep me here against my will. It's unlawful imprisonment." She stomps toward me but stops a few feet in front of me.

"Not kidnapping?" I tease as I close the gap between us.

"You don't appear intent on taking me to a different location."

I palm her cheek. "No, I'm not."

"What are you doing?" she asks, but her eyes dilate and she doesn't move away.

"I'm finally doing what I wanted to do the first time I saw you," I say as I stare at her pink lips.

"This is a bad idea."

"Do you want me to stop?"

"No," she whispers before she grasps the back of my neck and tugs my head down until my lips meet hers.

At the first touch of her soft lips against mine, I know I've made a mistake. Not because Lilac is an employee, but because I can easily become addicted to her lips. In fact, I may already be addicted to her taste of peppermint and cherries. Damn do I love cherries.

I wrap my arms around her and pull her near while I assume control of the kiss. I prod her lips until she opens, and my tongue pushes its way into heaven. She doesn't let me maintain control for long. Her tongue searches for mine and we duel for supremacy.

I groan and press my hardness against her stomach, and she freezes before dropping her hand and wrenching her lips from mine. She's gasping for breath, and her lips are swollen from my kisses. She's never been more beautiful.

But her eyes are wide and fearful. "This was a mistake. We shouldn't…You're my boss."

She clears her throat. "I'm sorry if I've led you on, but this can never happen again. Forget this ever happened."

"But…"

I don't have time to get my words out before she's throwing the door open and running down the hallway.

Well, shit. Our first kiss did not end the way I hoped it would.

Chapter 10

Literal – the use of words in a basic sense without exaggeration to indicate you're not messing around

I SWALLOW MY SIGH when I open the door to find my sisters in my hallway.

"What are you doing here?"

Aspen pushes her way past me. "I've got news."

"It's good." Ashlyn winks as she passes me.

I raise an eyebrow in question at Ellery and she pats my shoulder. "Don't ask me. My sole purpose in being here is to get a night off of baby duty."

Juniper rolls her eyes. "She's full of it. She already messaged Cole twice to check on Willow."

"I thought I was meeting you at the bar," I say.

Aspen wags her finger at me. "Don't think I don't know you were planning on ditching us."

"I wouldn't say ditching."

And I wouldn't. I don't use the term ditching. It's juvenile. But I can admit – if only to myself – I was not planning on joining them at the bar.

I barely survived book club without admitting I kissed Beckett. A night with alcohol involved is a bad idea. Besides, I have entirely too much work to finish. I glance at my dining room table where my laptop is open.

Ashlyn marches to my table and slams my computer shut. "There!"

"What are you doing?"

"Proving my hypothesis."

"What hypothesis?"

"Lilac Bean West is obsessed with work."

"Why am I getting the middle name treatment? And saying I'm obsessed with work is not a proper hypothesis. A hypothesis is about a relationship between two or more variables. It should be a specific and testable prediction of what will happen in a particular situation. You have no variables."

"I tried," Ashlyn mutters before collapsing on my couch. "Someone else is up to bat."

"I thought Aspen had news," I say before someone else can go 'up to bat'. I'm unsure what 'up to bat' means and I have no intention of finding out.

Aspen grins. "I do have news," she announces.

I wait a few seconds for her to continue, but when she doesn't, I ask, "Which is?"

"I'm getting married!"

"I'm confused. Why is this news? You've been engaged since September of last year."

"She means she set the date," Juniper explains. "Did you know this plant is sick? There are powdery blotches on the leaves."

"I am aware. You're not the only one with a master's degree in Biology."

Ashlyn groans. "Please tell me they're not going to geek out over plants now."

"I don't geek out of plants," Juniper claims.

"Uh-huh." Ashlyn rolls her eyes. "You leave the geeking out to your animals."

Although the terminology 'geek out' is somewhat offensive, it is true Juniper does tend to be slightly obsessive over animals. It's understandable as she manages the wildlife refuge. I would be concerned if she wasn't interested in animals.

"No!" Aspen warns. "We aren't going to discuss how Juniper's an animal freak or Lilac's an engineering freak or how Ellery works too much or how Ashlyn's a troublemaker."

"Hey! I can't help it if trouble finds me. I don't make it," Ashlyn claims.

Juniper snorts. "Because you're not the one who stole all the laundry from Feather's clothing line."

Ashlyn harrumphs. "Feather shouldn't have claimed her ice cream sundaes were better than Rowan's cakes. Everyone knows *Bake Me Happy* is the best bakery this side of the Mississippi. *Feather's Frozen Delights* can't compare. Besides, she got the chance to contact the police, and Peace showed up with his sweaty t-shirt molded to his chest. She should thank me for temporarily relieving her of her clothes."

"Didn't I literally just say we weren't going to discuss Ashlyn's troublemaking ways?" Aspen asks.

"I don't know. Lilac, did Aspen use the word literal correct in her question?" Ellery asks.

I narrow my eyes on her. "Are you being sarcastic?"

"Whoop! Whoop!" Ashlyn circles her arm in the air. "Lilac the literal understands sarcasm. Two points for Lilac. Zero for Aspen."

"Life isn't a competition," Aspen claims.

Ashlyn snorts. "It so is."

"In which case, I'm winning since I'm living with a movie star," Juniper claims.

If I was prone to rolling my eyes, I would at her proclamation. It took Juniper months to forgive Maverick Langston for what she thought he did and agree to move in with him.

"Why does living with a movie star make you the winner? I'm *married* to a former NFL quarterback with a Super Bowl ring who also makes the most delicious Red Velvet pancakes in the world."

Ellery moans in agreement. "His Red Velvet pancakes are to die for."

"Well, I'm married to the Chief of Police who can arrest all of you for annoying me."

"No, he can't," I tell Aspen. "Being annoying isn't a criminal offense for which the police can charge a person." If it were, my sisters would spend all of their time in jail.

Ashlyn wiggles her left hand toward Aspen and her diamond ring sparkles. "And you're not married."

"But I set a date. I'm as good as married."

"When are you getting married? I need to add the date to my calendar to ensure I have off or my boss will have me working late."

At the reminder of how working late ended up the other night, I feel my cheeks warm. Beckett's kiss is all I've been able to think about since it happened, which does not make me happy. Usually, I have perfect control over my emotions, but with Beckett, I feel out of control. He has too much influence over me.

Even if the man wasn't my boss, I wouldn't pursue a relationship with him. I need to be in control at all times and the one thing I am not in is control when it comes to Beckett.

"Is everyone seeing this?" Ashlyn asks and taps my cheek.

I rear back. When did she approach? And how did I not notice? This is why I can't be with Beckett. He messes with all my senses.

Juniper raises her hand. "I bear witness to this phenomenon."

"Me too!" Aspen also raises her hand.

"Yep!" Ellery's the last to raise her hand.

"What is going on now? What are you talking about?"

Normally, I don't understand when my sisters act this way, but I'm afraid I know the answer this time.

"Nuh-uh." Ashlyn wags her finger. "You're not getting away with crawling into your 'I don't understand what's going on'-hole."

"What is this hole? And where do I find it?"

She slaps my shoulder. "No. You can't pretend to be literal Lilac now when you understand what I'm talking about."

"She's correct," Aspen says as she stands next to Ashlyn.

They both study me as if I'm a specimen in a scientific experiment. Except I know for a fact Aspen never did a scientific experiment in her life. She avoided them in high school by pulling the fire alarm.

It was extremely agitating since I was in all of her high school science classes despite being four years her junior. Although I should probably thank her as I learned to perform those experiments with the blare of a fire alarm in the background. It did wonders for my concentration.

Ellery sighs from her place on my sofa. "You might as well tell them why you're blushing, or we'll be here all night while they beat it out of you."

"Beat it out of me?"

"She's not being literal. Duh." Ashlyn rolls her eyes.

"I, for one, don't need to hear what Lilac has to say," Juniper announces.

"You don't? Are you feeling okay? Oh wait. Is this some newfangled idea of 'privacy' since you're now engaged to a movie star?" Ashlyn feigns gagging.

"One, we're not engaged."

"Yet," Ellery tags on.

Juniper ignores Ellery's interruption. "And, two, I don't need to know because I already do."

My mouth gapes open and words rush out before I have the chance to think. "How in the world do you know I kissed my boss at work?"

Juniper smiles in triumph, and I realize she tricked me. Damn Beckett. This is all his fault. Usually, my sisters are incapable of tricking me in any manner.

"High five!" Ellery lifts her hand and Juniper smacks it. "Awesome job."

Juniper bows. "Thank you."

"I didn't see this coming," Aspen mutters.

Ashlyn elbows her. "You didn't? You're the chairperson of the committee to match Lilac with Beckett."

I sincerely hope my baby sister is exaggerating and there is no committee to match me with my boss.

"Yeah, but I thought we'd need months to get to this juncture."

"It has been months. Beckett took over the CEO position at *Clean Mountain Environment* a year ago." Ellery waves her phone at Aspen. "It says as much on their website."

"This is awesome!" Ashlyn cheers. "We know something before the gossip gals."

"This is not awesome," I hiss. "I could lose my job."

She waves away my concern. "You've got it all wrong. Grumpy boss romances go as follows: boss is grumpy, but the subordinate – you in this instance – smashes through their defenses and they end up fooling around and falling in love. Everything works out in the end."

I glare at her. "You do realize my life is not one of those romance novels you narrate."

Ashlyn studied drama in college but instead of going to Hollywood to star in films, she decided to become an audiobook narrator. She is now a known narrator for sexy romance novels. Her husband even built her a studio, *Bertie's Recording Studio,* in town.

"But it could be," she sings.

"Are you worried about your job?" Juniper asks before I have a chance to lecture Ashlyn on the difference between fiction and reality.

What an absurd question. Of course, I'm worried. "There is a no fraternization policy at our office."

"Is Beckett your direct supervisor? If he's not, maybe there's wiggle room in the policy," Ellery suggests.

"There is no wiggle room."

She frowns. "I hate to say it, but you need to nip this in the bud."

"She means you should stop kissing Beckett before the situation worsens," Juniper explains.

"I am familiar with the expression 'nip in the bud'." Although this is my first time actually saying the phrase since idioms can be misinterpreted and there is nothing worse than a misunderstanding.

"Are we advising her to ignore Beckett and the chemistry between them?" Ashlyn's gaze bounces back and forth between Ellery, Aspen, and Juniper. "You've got to be joking."

Juniper stands. "I'm not joking. Getting fired would hurt Lilac's career and her career is important to her."

Ashlyn's nose wrinkles. "Is this one of those reverse psychology thingies? We're telling her to avoid him, so all she can do is think about him."

Juniper fast blinks. "Of course not."

I narrow my eyes on her. I'm unsure as to whether she's being truthful.

Aspen pats my shoulder. "Alrighty. You just avoid Mr. Grumpy Boss, and all will be well." She motions toward the door, and everyone follows her.

When I set the alarm after they depart, I'm frowning. Were they being serious? All I need to do is avoid Beckett? On the surface, it appears to be a simple solution, but I can't avoid my boss at work. It's not professional.

Why did Beckett Dempsey have to show up at *Clean Mountain Environment?* I was perfectly content before he arrived. I had my career, my family, and various male companionship when I felt the need for sexual release.

But now I don't want any other male companionship than Beckett. And my career is in jeopardy because of it. I knew Beckett was complicated. I didn't realize he was trouble.

Chapter 11

Stubborn – determination to hold your course despite having good reasons not to do so

"You're driving with me to the meeting," Beckett barks from my office doorway.

I startle and nearly fall off my chair. I used to always shut my door while I was concentrating on a project to avoid this type of interruption, but Beckett commanded everyone keep their office doors open at all times.

When I asked the company lawyer to review this policy as I feel it's an invasion of privacy, he laughed at me. I still don't understand what's funny. And why does everyone seem to be laughing at me lately?

I dig my fingernails into the arms of my chair before I can give into temptation and stand to slam the door in his face.

"I am not driving with you. I have somewhere to be after the meeting."

He growls. "Another date."

I consider lying and saying I do have a date when the 'somewhere' I have to be after the meeting is actually a location in town Aspen's considering for her wedding venue. Although,

I'm confused as to why we're reviewing venues in White Bridge. Aspen will have her wedding reception in Winter Falls at the bar, *Electric Vibes*. There's no way our parents will allow anything else.

The fact I'm considering lying is an indication of the effect Beckett has on me. I never lie. Although, I sometimes lie on behalf of my sisters. But they must request I lie beforehand and provide a detailed analysis of why the lie is necessary. Unlike they claim, I don't require the request in triplicate.

"As we discussed, my private life is my own and you are not allowed to ask me questions about it." I straighten my back as satisfaction fills me at my answer. I didn't lie, but he doesn't know the truth either.

"It's my business if it's during work hours."

"I have the right to a one-hour lunch break every full working day. The lunch break can be enjoyed at any time of the day between 8 a.m. and 5 p.m."

His nostrils flare. "There's no need to quote the employee manual to me."

I frown. "Are you certain? It appears you don't have the in-depth knowledge of the manual as you should as CEO."

He steps into the office and shuts the door behind him.

"Open the door!" When I realize I screeched, I clear my throat and say in a much calmer voice, "Open the door, please. I don't want it to appear to the rest of the employees as if there is anything inappropriate happening in here."

"Inappropriate like the kiss we shared?"

I purse my lips. "We agreed to pretend the kiss never happened."

"No. You said, 'forget this ever happened'. I never agreed to forget it." He prowls closer. "Because I can't forget it."

I cross my arms over my chest. No, this is a defensive stance. There's no need for me to be defensive. I'm not in the wrong here. I drop my arms and grasp the edge of my desk.

"We can't be in a relationship. The employee handbook specifically forbids fraternization between employees."

He lays his palms flat on my desk and leans over. "I'm not an employee."

"On the contrary, the Chief Executive Officer is considered an employee of the company."

He opens his mouth to argue with me but snaps it closed again before pushing off from my desk and straightening his tie. "Yes, of course. You are correct as always."

I wait until his footsteps fade away before I slump in my chair. Maybe my sisters and their juvenile approach to my problem is correct. Maybe I should avoid Beckett until whatever chemistry between us dies out. If I'm not in his vicinity, his overwhelming presence can't affect me. And I won't end up doing something foolish such as kissing him again.

When I arrive at the client's office building thirty minutes later, I park next to Beckett's car in the visitor parking lot. I climb out of my car and my boss follows suit.

I ball my hands in frustration. He couldn't have gone inside the building ahead of me? He has to escort me inside? I'm a full-grown woman, not a child.

"Beckett." I nod to him in greeting, and he grunts in response. I sigh. Is he not speaking to me now?

We arrive at the door, and he reaches forward to open it for me. While I walk through, he places a hand on my lower back to guide me inside. The feel of his strong hand on my back causes a jolt of electricity to run through me and I end up tripping.

Beckett steadies me with a hand on my elbow. "You okay?" he whispers in my ear.

My body is officially on overload. My skin burns from his touch and goosebumps spread from my ear down my neck at the feel of his breath against my skin.

"I need the restroom. I'll meet you in the conference room," I say before rushing away.

I hurry down a hallway until I reach the women's restroom. I slam the door closed behind me and lock it before leaning against it while I try to catch my breath.

This is ridiculous. My body should not have such a visceral response to Beckett's. Sexual chemistry and attractiveness have no objective criteria making them immeasurable and completely subjective, which means I should be able to control my body's response to my boss. But I can't.

I wet some paper towels and wipe my forehead with them. When I check my watch, I realize I don't have time to waste. I need to get to my meeting post-haste.

I return to the reception area, but Beckett is gone as is the receptionist. I tap my foot as I wait for her return, but after waiting a minute, I decide I can delay no longer. I'll find the conference room on my own. It can't be difficult.

I march to the elevators, but there isn't a plan of the building. I scan the surrounding area. Shouldn't there be a plan in case of an emergency?

The elevators open and a man exits.

"Excuse me. Where are the conference rooms?"

"Top floor."

I smile my thanks before hopping into the vacant elevator. I push the button for the eleventh floor.

Calm down, Lilac. The meeting starts in seven minutes. You're not late.

I consult my watch again. Six minutes and fifty seconds. I blow out a breath of air. I have plenty of time.

The elevator doors open, and I step into the hallway. I'm on a small landing with one door directly ahead of me. I smooth my blouse down and straighten my back before pushing the door open and marching through.

The smile affixed to my face freezes when I realize I'm on the roof. I whirl around to catch the door before it closes but it slams shut in front of my eyes. Perhaps it's not locked, although being unlocked would be an egregious security breach.

I try the door but as I suspected, it's locked. I remove my phone from my pocket and dial Beckett's number. He doesn't answer. Of all the times for him to start ignoring me, it has to be now when I need him.

Think, Lilac. Think.

I need to work out a solution, but I'm not going to work anything out standing on the rooftop glaring at my phone. I should perform a reconnaissance. To my right is the edge of the roof and the street. As I'm unable to fly, this is unhelpful information. Behind me is the locked door. Also unhelpful.

I head to the left and discover a panel of skylights jutting out of the roof. I tiptoe closer in order to peer into the windows and realize this is the conference room I've been searching for. Beckett as well as several representatives of the client are mulling about.

Good. The meeting hasn't started yet. I check my watch. I have two minutes to make it into the room. But how?

I phone Beckett once more, but he ignores the call again. Why is he ignoring my calls? He knows I should be in the meeting and I'm somewhere in the building.

Is he trying to sabotage my career? Does he want to fire me? Did he kiss me to have a reason to fire me?

No. No. And no. *You're being utterly ridiculous, Lilac.* None of those theories is remotely possible. And his kiss couldn't have been faked. He can't fake his hard dick pushing against my stomach.

Perhaps he doesn't want to interrupt his discussion with the client. Yes, this makes much more sense. I'll send a message instead.

I need your assistance. I'm stuck on the roof.

I hit send and watch as Beckett looks down at his phone. His eyes widen when he reads my message, and he lifts his gaze skyward. I wave and he returns the gesture.

Unfortunately, the other participants at the meeting notice him waving at the roof and gaze upwards as well. I smile at them before backing away.

"What are you doing on the roof?" Beckett asks when he opens the door for me a minute later. I expect him to bark out his question – I am embarrassing our company after all – but his lips are tipped up in a barely there smile.

"I was told the conference room was on the top floor. I wasn't made aware of the elevator going to the roof level."

The barely there smile becomes a full blown one. "Only you would remain calm and have a reasonable explanation for getting stuck on the roof."

"Because there is a reasonable explanation."

He grasps my elbow and leads me into the elevator. "We'll tell the client you were examining the energy efficiency of the glass roof."

"You want me to lie? I don't lie."

"You can't tell me your humongous brain didn't review the skylights the second you saw them."

Of course, I did but, "If you're trying to say a humongous brain is a compliment, you should know brain size only weakly correlates with intelligence. Brain size accounts for—"

"We're here," he cuts me off as he opens the door to the conference room. "Good news. I found our environmental engineer. She was on the roof analyzing your skylights."

He winks at me before introducing me around. I stare after him. Do I thank him for saving me from a potentially embarrassing situation? Embarrassing situations don't phase me, but he was trying to be helpful, which means I have to thank him. I think.

Human relationships are confusing. Especially when the relationship is with a boss who kisses you and refuses to pretend said kiss didn't happen.

Chapter 12

Boss – someone who thinks he's in charge of your life

BECKETT

"Why are we here?" Cassandra asks.

We're in Winter Falls for their Litha festival, but I'm not telling her the real reason we're here. Instead, I avoid her question by asking one of my own. "You don't want to go to a pagan festival?"

"You know I do. What I don't know is why all three of us had to come with you today."

"I get it!" Elizabeth proclaims before slamming a hand over her mouth.

Gabrielle giggles but quickly hides her mirth by tucking her chin into her chest and concealing her face behind her hair. I frown. My youngest sister has always been shy, but in the past year since we moved to Colorado, she's been acting painfully shy. It's almost as if she's afraid of something.

I throw my arm over her and bring her near. "What are you giggling about?" I tease.

She points toward the crowd, and I follow her finger to discover Lilac glaring at me. When our eyes meet, she scowls before stomping over to us.

"You're invading my private life again," she accuses.

"Who says I'm here to see you? Maybe I brought my sisters to Winter Falls to observe the Litha festival."

I hold my breath while I wait to learn if she bought my lie. Her shoulders relax. "Oh. Okay then."

She whirls around to run away, but I shackle her wrist to stop her.

"As long as you're here, though, maybe you can tell us what this Litha festival is all about."

She stares at my fingers on her arm for a moment and I can't resist rubbing circles into the soft skin on the inside of her wrist with my thumb. She yanks her hand out of my hold but not before I feel her shiver.

"I don't think—"

"I want to know more about Litha," Gabrielle says. Did my shy sister just act as my wingwoman?

"Me, too," Elizabeth hurries to agree.

"Oh, I want to know about a little something-something," Cassandra mutters.

Lilac frowns at Cassandra before explaining, "Litha is also known as Midsummer or the Summer Solstice. It marks an important transitional moment in the Earth's seasonal cycle. Fertile energy is at its peak and new life is rapidly growing. Seeds have been sown and begin to grow in abundance until Lughnasadh, which is the first harvest."

"And how do you celebrate Litha?" Gabrielle asks.

"Not by sacrificing one of my goats at an altar," a man answers as he passes us with a goat on a leash. I fast blink, but I'm not hallucinating. He's leading an actual goat around on a leash.

The goat bleats before lunging for Gabrielle. No, not for Gabrielle. For her skirt. She giggles as the goat latches onto the hem.

"You're a bad goat," she coos as she pets him.

The man rushes to her and pulls the goat away except the goat refuses to release Gabrielle's skirt. She's dragged forward as they both attempt to loosen his teeth from her skirt. "Knock it off, Pan, or you won't get any watermelon."

At the word watermelon, the goat releases Gabrielle's skirt and she flies backward. The man catches her before she can fall.

"You okay? I'm sorry Pan accosted you."

Gabrielle blushes but holds his gaze. "Pan didn't accost me. She's a sweet thing, aren't you?"

Pan proves her wrong by butting her hand, but Gabrielle scratches behind her ears like Pan's a dog and not a goat.

Before the man can respond, Lilac interrupts, "Phoenix, it's not appropriate for your goat to eat the skirts of tourists."

"It's not his fault I'm wearing a hemp skirt today," Gabrielle defends the complete stranger and surprises the shit out of me.

"Thanks." Phoenix grins at Gabrielle. "But she's not wrong. Pan here is a pain in my ass." He leans down and scratches the goat under her chin. "Aren't you, girl?"

Phoenix and Gabrielle pet the goat together while grinning at each other.

"I heard altar. Are we sacrificing to the gods?" Cassandra rubs her hands together in excitement.

Lilac huffs. "There is not an altar."

"Because Ms. Fussy Pants won't let us have one. But if we're sacrificing to the gods, I vote we sacrifice Love Hill," one of Lilac's sisters says as she joins us.

"Who's Love Hill?" Cassandra asks. "And do we need to glitter bomb her?"

I ignore Cassandra and extend my hand to Lilac's sister. "Ashlyn, isn't it?"

She winks as she shakes my hand. "And you're Beckett, the grumpy boss."

Cassandra laughs. "We call him grumpasauras, the last living dinosaur."

"Love it!" Ashlyn grabs Cassandra and Elizabeth's hands. "Come on. Let's leave the love birds alone."

"Whenever Ashlyn is up to her scheming, it's my cue to exit stage left. I have no desire to wake up to my goats wearing skirts and bikini tops again." Phoenix shivers before tugging on the goat's leash. "See ya around," he says and saunters away.

Gabrielle watches him walk away while biting her lip. Maybe she's not as afraid of men as I thought.

"You, too," Ashlyn barks at her, and Gabrielle jumps. "I want you to meet my sisters."

Ashlyn hauls Cassandra and Elizabeth away while Gabrielle trails after them.

Lilac stares after them. "I don't believe it's a good idea for Ashlyn and Cassandra to meet."

"They'll be fine," I say since I don't want to talk about our sisters.

She purses her lips. "I'm not worried about them. I'm worried about the town."

I throw my arm over her shoulders and indicate the festivities happening around us. "Forget about them and show me around your town."

She leans into me for a moment before remembering herself and shoving me away. "You're my boss," she hisses.

"We're not at work."

She rolls her eyes. "I'm aware. You are still my boss even if we aren't at work."

"But we aren't at work, so we can let our hair down."

She pats her hair, which isn't in the tight bun she favors at work and is instead flowing down her back tempting me to fist my hands in it.

"I concede your point, but we shouldn't touch each other. I don't want you to get the wrong idea."

I step closer. "And what's the wrong idea?"

"Are you deliberately being obtuse?"

"Maybe I want to hear your opinion."

"My opinion?" Her brows furrow. "The company employee manual contains a no fraternization rule. This is not an opinion. It's a fact."

"Good thing being friends isn't fraternization then." I motion to the crowd up ahead. "Lead the way."

She hesitates for a moment before she begins walking. "Litha is a celebration of the fertility of the gods and is often celebrated with a bonfire."

I scan the area. "I don't see a bonfire."

"Because there isn't one. You should know how bad bonfires are for the environment."

I ignore her chastisement. Her opinion on my knowledge of the environment is not news. She made it perfectly clear what she thought of my lack of an environmental engineering degree when I took over the position of CEO at *Clean Mountain Environment.*

"If there's no bonfire, how do you celebrate?"

"In addition to the street fair." She motions to the various vendors lining the sides of the street. "We have a drum circle dance, and we jump over the bonfire."

"Hold up. You just said there's no bonfire."

"Winter Falls doesn't allow anything – including a ban on bonfires – to stop it from carrying out pagan traditions."

"This I've got to see."

She checks her watch. "I believe they're about to begin. Come along."

I follow her through the crowd until we reach the town square. Two poles are set up in the middle of the square with a pile of hay in between them.

"Is the hay the bonfire?"

"We used candles in the past but after Forest attempted to set a new jumping record and ended up burning his t-shirt in the process, we decided to use strictly non-flammable items."

"Set a new jumping record? Is jumping over the bonfire a contest?"

"It is and because I was unsuccessful in passing the no gambling legislation, it's also high stakes."

"No gambling legislation?"

"Nope," Ashlyn yells as she joins us. "No lecturing about how we bet too much. It does no one any harm."

"Except Forest ruined his favorite t-shirt and got second degree burns on his back."

"Come on. You're jumping." Ashlyn shoves her sister, but Lilac plants her feet.

"I do not jump. I'm judging."

"I agreed with Rowan I wouldn't jump as long as you act as my proxy."

"Who's Rowan?" I ask.

She indicates a man across the street. He has his arms crossed over his massive chest as he glares our way. "My baby daddy. Which is why I can't jump." She rolls her eyes. "According to him, I shouldn't be doing 'strenuous' activities while I'm pregnant. Good thing sex isn't considered strenuous." She winks. "Although the way we do it is."

"Why can't Aspen be your proxy?" Lilac asks before I can manage to figure out a way to respond to Ashlyn.

"Duh. Aspen's my rival. And it's up to you to kick her butt."

"Me? Maybe you should ask Beckett's sister, Cassandra."

Ashlyn indicates the line Cassandra is already standing in. "She wants to win on her own."

"I'll be your proxy," I tell Ashlyn, knowing damn well Lilac will see my offer as an attempt to interfere.

"No, you won't," Lilac says, and I cough to hide my smile. "I'll do it." She hands Ashlyn the clipboard she's carrying. "But you have to judge, and you won't play favorites."

Ashlyn lifts two fingers in the air. "Scout's promise."

"You were never a scout."

"It's not my fault they didn't understand my vision."

"Storming the police station is not a vision."

"You stormed the police station?" I ask.

Ashlyn waves away my concern. "It was a misunderstanding." She grasps Lilac's shoulders and pushes her toward the line. "Do your best. I understand if you can't beat my record."

Lilac bristles. Her sister knows her well. She hates being told she isn't good at something. I get in line behind her because I am not missing this.

As we wait, everyone in line has a turn at jumping as high as they can over the 'bonfire'. Next to me, Lilac drums her fingers against her thigh. It's her nervous tell. I want to grasp her hand and tell her it's going to be fine, but I know my touch isn't welcomed. Especially not when we're in public.

I plan to change how Lilac feels, but first I have to figure out what she wants. Avoiding me because of an employee handbook is not an answer.

"You got this," I tell her when she's next. I take a chance and squeeze her shoulder in support.

"Okay. Okay. I can do this," she mutters to herself.

She backs up several steps before sprinting toward the hay pile. A foot in front of the pile, she trips and flies through the air before landing on top of the hay.

I rush forward to ensure she isn't injured. When I reach her, she smiles up at me with hay in her hair and giggles. "I fell."

Trouble. It's the one and only word I can think of as I stare down at her smiling face.

I'm in trouble. I thought I was in trouble with Lilac the hard working professional. I was wrong. Lilac the woman who will make a fool out of herself for her family is the real trouble. Good thing I enjoy trouble.

Chapter 13

Silence falling – an indication shit is about to get real

I ENTER MY PARENTS' house for Sunday dinner, and silence falls upon the room. My lips purse as I study the members of my family – none of whom will meet my gaze.

I may be awkward in social situations and not always understand when someone is being sarcastic, but I do know when people were talking about me. Refusing to look me in the eyes is one of the indicators. Studying sociology while working on my engineering degree helped me to understand my social awkwardness as well as learn to appraise social situations.

"What are you hiding from me?"

"Nothing," Mom claims.

I cross my arms over my chest and lift an eyebrow. Mom may be the sneakiest mother I know – I am unaware of any other people who had to endure their mother planting condoms in their purses when they were teenagers – but she is a horrible liar.

"The sex of the baby!" Ashlyn blurts out.

According to my quick calculations, Ashlyn is just entering her second trimester. "You should be able to have an ultrasound to determine the baby's gender with nearly one-hundred percent accuracy now."

"Yes, but should we? Or do we want it to be a surprise?" She bites her lip as she pretends to consider her choices.

"You want it to be a surprise," I tell her because I know my sister. "Or rather, you want to know what the gender is, but you don't want anyone else to know. However, you can't keep a secret and will end up telling everyone anyway."

Her mouth drops open before she snaps it shut and narrows her eyes on me. "Can you read my mind? Wait! Did you plant a chip in my brain?"

"I think you're confused as to what type of engineer I am. I don't plant chips into brains."

She wags a finger at me. "So, you don't deny being able to read my mind?"

"Telepathy does not exist. I've explained this to you before."

"You got to admit if anyone could figure out how to read minds, it would be you."

"Why would it be me? Do I need to explain to you what an environmental engineer does again?"

She moans. "No, not the PowerPoint. Anything but the PowerPoint."

"My PowerPoint presentations are clear and concise." I'm quite proud of them.

"Of course, they are, dear," Mom says and squeezes my hand.

I stare at her hand on mine, and she immediately yanks hers away. I frown. I didn't mean for her to yank her hand away.

I'm merely confused as to why she's comforting me. There's no reason to comfort me unless—

"Not only were you talking about me when I arrived, you were specifically discussing my sex life."

"I told you she'd figure it out," Aspen mutters.

"Figure what out? I've told you about my sex life in the past. It isn't a surprise."

Ashlyn groans and covers her face with her hands. "Not again. I don't need to hear about my sister's sex life."

"I'm confused. You always tell everyone about your sex life. Why do you maintain a double standard?"

Rowan removes Ashlyn's hands from her face and taps her nose. "Because someone knows it makes everyone uncomfortable when she brings up her sex life."

"It doesn't make me uncomfortable. I'm quite aware my baby sister has a sex life. She is pregnant after all." Ashlyn sticks her tongue out at me. I ignore her childish behavior. "Now, what about my sex life were you discussing?"

"I vote we leave her alone," Lyric says before raising his hand.

"I agree," Rowan says and raises his hand.

I scan the room and note all of the men in the room – Lyric, Rowan, Cole, and Dad – have their hands raised while my sisters and Mom refuse to meet my gaze. I add up the clues – they were talking about me, the men think they should leave me alone, and the women don't agree. The conclusion is obvious.

"Why are you trying to matchmake me?"

"I, for one, am bored out of my mind. Having a boyfriend who's away shooting a film for three months straight is no fun," Juniper grumbles.

"I offered to let you babysit," Ellery says.

"Mom won't let me."

"Willow is my grandchild. If anyone's babysitting her, it's me."

Ashlyn rubs her hands together. "This is awesome. When our baby's born, she'll babysit him or her, too."

Juniper stomps her foot. "I'm your baby's godmother, I declare I will have equal babysitting rights as the baby's grandmother."

While my sisters and Mom discuss the grandchildren, Dad comes over and wraps his arm around my shoulder.

"You okay, baby girl?"

"Of course, I'm okay. Why wouldn't I be?"

He chuckles. "No reason, darling. No reason."

I study him. When Dad says no reason, he really means there is a reason. Maybe I didn't add up the clues correctly after all. My family wants to matchmake me and yesterday I was with—

"No," I say when I realize what's happening.

"Told you," Ellery sings as she rocks Willow in her arms.

"You're such a fuddy-duddy," Aspen accuses.

"No, I'm not. I understand Lilac's hesitation to get involved with her boss. If things don't work out, it would be awkward for her at work."

"Have you met our sister?" Aspen asks. "She doesn't do awkward."

Ellery passes the baby to Cole before confronting Aspen. "Are you kidding? Lilac is the definition of awkward."

I clear my throat. This is my chance to derail their conversation. "Awkward means—"

Ellery shoves a hand in my face. "I know what awkward means. You know what awkward means. We all know what awkward means." She lowers her hand and meets my gaze. "I also know you knew what I meant and interrupted me because you're uncomfortable with where the conversation is going."

My brow furrows. Does my sister understand me? Have I underestimated her?

Silence falls until Ellery says, "Dating your boss is a bad idea."

"None of you read enough romance books. In romance books, dating your boss always works out," Ashlyn says.

"Must I state the obvious?" I ask. When no one responds, I continue, "This is not a romance book. My life is real."

Mom claps her hands. "Good. The matter's settled then."

When Mom says the matter is settled, what she really means is she's going to ignore your side of the story and do whatever she wants.

"I believe it's time to eat."

"I'm starving," Ashlyn announces as she bounces toward the dining table. "Oh no!" she screams and everyone rushes after her. She flails her hands toward the table.

Ellery's puppy, Honey, is standing in the middle of the table eating the meatloaf. Cole rushes forward and grabs for her, but the pup slips out of his hold and jumps off the table before running away with a mouthful of meatloaf.

"I think I'll skip Sunday dinner this week," I state as I stare at the mess the puppy made of the table.

"Why was your puppy here today?" Aspen asks. "I don't get to bring Waffles with me."

Waffles is Aspen's rescue dog she brought home from Dallas. All of my sisters are animal lovers, although Juniper is the only one who has made her love of animals into a profession.

I, for one, don't understand the appeal of having an animal. They're messy, need to be fed and walked, and shed fur everywhere.

"Girls! Can we not argue about who gets to bring what animal to Sunday dinner now? We need to clean this mess up." Mom picks up the remaining meatloaf and marches to the kitchen.

"You're not going to throw food away, are you?" Juniper asks as she follows her. "My dogs love meatloaf."

"I'm glad I don't live with her anymore," Ashlyn mutters. "Her dogs may love meatloaf, but they also love to throw up after they eat human food. She should know better."

Dad elbows me. "Go on. This is your chance to escape."

I know better than to run out of a family meal, even if such meal has been ruined by a rambunctious puppy. "But Mom."

"I'll deal with your mother. I have my methods."

He waggles his eyebrows in case I was confused about what methods he would use. I wasn't confused. My parents have a very active sex life, which they never tried to hide from us when we were children. I know exactly how Dad settles Mom down.

"Thank you." He winks and I make my way out of the house.

As I bike home, I analyze the interactions of my family today and in the past. I think I am beginning to understand why my sisters attempted to avoid Sunday dinners when they were having relationship problems with men. It's not enjoyable to have the entire family involved in your business.

But my family is confused about the situation. Beckett and I aren't involved. He's my boss. I'm not worried about work becoming awkward. I'm worried about losing my job. I've worked entirely too hard at my career to get fired over a man.

Chapter 14

Misunderstanding – when two people aren't using the same terminology and get into a fight about it

"Here's the key to your room," the receptionist says and hands Beckett two key cards. He smiles at me before nodding to the person behind me.

"Excuse me, I was here first. Can you check me in now?" I interrupt before he can greet the other customer.

"I checked you in."

"No, you didn't. You checked Mr. Dempsey in. I'm Ms. West."

His brow furrows as he consults his computer. "I only have one room reserved for *Clean Mountain Environment*."

"There must be a mistake. We'll need two rooms for the night."

"I'm sorry, but we're fully booked due to the convention."

"Can you recommend another hotel?"

Before the receptionist has a chance to respond, Beckett tags my hand and drags me away.

"What is wrong with you?" I ask when I manage to free my hand from his. "I'm trying to fix the mistake your PA made.

You can rest assured I'll be mentioning this to her when we return to White Bridge. This type of mistake is completely unacceptable."

"You won't be mentioning anything to Brandi," he growls, and tingles erupt in my core at the sound.

I ignore the feeling. This is not the appropriate time for my sexual attraction to the man to make itself known.

"Fine. Do it yourself. It doesn't matter. Now, can I go find a hotel room? I'm tired and my feet hurt."

I whirl around to march to the reception desk, but Beckett shackles my wrist to stop me. He rubs his thumb in circles over my skin and the tingles in my core multiply until I feel a warmth spread throughout my body.

I yank my hand out of his grasp and retreat several feet. Distance is what I need. Distance will ensure I don't act on this ridiculous chemistry between us.

"Stop it."

He smirks. "Stop what?"

"I don't want to play games with you. You know exactly what I mean." I wait until he nods in understanding before continuing, "I'm going to fix this mess. I'll see you tomorrow."

I stride to the receptionist's desk with Beckett on my heels. Of course, he doesn't let me be. Since the Litha festival, he hasn't left me alone. He's pushed and pushed and pushed. I should have never let my hair down with him – literally or figuratively. I have learned my lesson and filed the information away for future encounters.

"I'm sorry," the receptionist says when it's finally my turn again. "I've contacted every hotel in the downtown area. No one has any openings this evening."

"Every hotel? It's highly unlikely every single hotel room in San Francisco is booked. There are 34,000 hotel rooms in this city. There must be an available room somewhere."

"Maybe I can find a hotel room in Oakland for you?" he suggests.

"No," Beckett barks. "You're not staying in Oakland."

"Why not? I admit Oakland is the tenth most dangerous metro city in the country with a crime rate four times higher than the national average, but I won't be strolling down the city streets in the middle of the night. I will be safely secure in my hotel room the entire time."

He rubs a hand down his face. "The tenth most dangerous metro city in the country? I don't think so."

I frown. "Do you contend my data is incorrect?"

"No, I contend you staying in a hotel in the tenth most dangerous metro city in the country."

I ignore him to tell the receptionist, "Your suggestion is acceptable. Could you please procure me a hotel room in Oakland?"

"Over my dead body," Beckett grumbles before hauling me away once again.

"What is wrong with you?" I hiss at him. "The receptionist will think I'm an indecisive woman."

"The receptionist doesn't think you're an indecisive woman."

"How do you know?"

He points to the receptionist who's waving and giving Beckett a thumbs-up.

"Why is he giving you a thumbs-up?"

Beckett shrugs, which is a convenient way to lie without actually speaking words.

"It doesn't matter. What matters is I won't allow you to drive all the way to Oakland to stay in a hotel there when you have an important presentation tomorrow morning."

I bristle. "Are you doubting my capabilities again?" The tingles in my core evaporate as anger replaces excitement.

"Again? What do you…" He cuts himself off. "Never mind. You'll stay in my room."

"Do you have two beds?"

"No. There's one bed."

"Where will you sleep?"

"I can sleep in bed with you."

Those tingles flare back to life. I place a hand on my stomach and inhale a deep breath. I know better than to allow the chemistry between us ruin my career.

"Your proposal is unacceptable. I'll sleep on the floor."

"You are not sleeping on the floor," he growls.

I cross my arms over my chest and his gaze dips to my cleavage before he clears his voice and glances away. His display of sexual attraction to me is confirmation I'm correct. We can't stay in a hotel room together.

"Since I'm not sleeping in a bed with you and you won't sleep on the floor and you won't let me sleep on the floor, the only solution is for me to get a hotel room in Oakland."

"I don't know why you're making such a big deal about this. You've slept with plenty of men."

What is he talking about? Why is he abruptly changing the subject? "No, I haven't."

"You haven't?" He crosses his arms over his chest. "It wasn't you I caught sneaking into a hotel room in Arkville with a man?"

"Arkville? Sneaking into a hotel room? What are you talking about? Have you been spying on me?"

"It's not spying if it's not deliberate."

"While I do not completely agree with your definition of the word spy, it's immaterial as I haven't slept with any man in Arkville."

He bends down slightly until he can meet my gaze. "I saw you."

"I don't know what you saw but I don't sleep with men."

"I saw you," he repeats.

I think back on my encounters in Arkville. It's been a while since I spent any time there as Beckett has been successful in ensuring I'm too busy to escape the office for an hour-long lunch regardless of whether I have a right to one or not. The last time I was there—

Oh wait. He's not talking about me sleeping with men. He's talking about me having sex with men. He should have made himself clear.

"There's been a misunderstanding."

"I didn't misunderstand what I saw."

"Can I continue?" I ask but don't wait for his reply. "I didn't realize you were using 'sleep' as a euphemism for sex. I am sometimes too literal in my interpretation of words and phrases and since we are talking about sleeping in the same bed, I assumed you meant sleep and not sex."

He blows a breath of air, and his shoulders relax. "I should have been clearer."

"It's fine. It's my fault for not asking for clarification."

"To be perfectly clear, then, what you're saying is you don't sleep with men?"

"Correct. Sharing a bed with a man is too intimate."

"Okay. I'll sleep on the floor."

"What? Why are you changing your mind now?"

"I just am." He grasps my hand and leads me to the elevators. "Come on. Let's get changed and order room service."

"Room service is ridiculously priced. We can eat in the bar."

"Good thing the boss is footing the bill."

"True, but my boss is a stickler who reviews every single item on my expense claim."

He screeches to a stop in the lobby of the hotel and grins down at me. "Lilac West, are you teasing me?"

I roll my eyes. "I do know how to tease someone. I did grow up with four sisters after all."

"Tell me about it. I brought up my four sisters," he grumbles as he resumes walking.

"And you did a remarkable job." At least with regard to the three sisters I've met.

"Handing out compliments now, are you?"

He winks and those delicious tingles return along with a jolt of anticipation. I take a deep breath and ignore the desire to jump Beckett in the elevator. I don't care how many romantic books Aspen makes me read. There is no way I'll ever believe you can have any type of sexual encounter in an elevator without being caught.

I frown at those thoughts. I'm not having a sexual encounter with Beckett because he's my boss and being with him risks my career. My decision has nothing to do with the likelihood of being spotted in an elevator with my pants down.

The elevator pings and the doors open. My shoulders fall in relief when I notice the crowd in the compartment. Beckett drops my hand and motions for me to go ahead. I scurry into the corner where there's barely enough room for one person, let alone two.

He smirks and I realize staying overnight in a room with him could be the biggest mistake of my life, but what can I do? Sneak out in the middle of the night?

Sneaking out will not help with the performance of my presentation in the morning. I'll have to figure out a way to put figurative space between us when the actual space is limited.

Chapter 15

Embarrass – to cause someone to feel awkward – assuming the person has the ability to feel awkward

BECKETT

I hide my grin when I open the door to *our* hotel room for the night. I shouldn't be amused watching the tension roll off Lilac in waves, but she always appears so cool and composed. It's a relief to discover she can get flustered.

I know she's worried about what will happen to her career if we become romantically involved. What she doesn't know is I would never let anything hurt her career. And now that I know those men, I saw her with, meant nothing to her, nothing will stop me from having her.

I follow her into the room. It's a typical hotel room with a desk and chair against the wall next to a large flat screen television and a round table with two chairs near the window. Smack dab in the middle of the room is an extra-large bed. It's big enough for both of us to sleep in without touching.

Not touching is not what either one of us wants, no matter what Lilac claims. The chemistry between us buzzes at such an intensity in the air whenever we're near each other that it's practically visible. She's doing a stellar job of ignoring it, but I'm done ignoring it. I just have to figure out how to convince her I'm worth taking a chance on.

"Do you want to use the bathroom first?"

At my question, she startles from where she's standing staring at the bed and spins around. "Yes, thank you."

She rushes off and slams the door behind her. I grin at the closed door. I'm enjoying experiencing her off-kilter. Lilac is never off-kilter. She's even keeled and in charge at all times. I have plans to mess with her steadiness every chance I get.

If she were any other woman, I'd expect her to hide in the bathroom and avoid the situation until morning. But not my Lilac. She doesn't hide from anything.

I scan the room service menu before placing an order with the kitchen.

"Our food will be here in fifteen minutes," I tell Lilac through the door.

It opens and my eyes widen in surprise at how she's dressed. My cock immediately takes notice and begins to harden.

Shit. I'm going to have to give my incompetent PA a raise for screwing up and forgetting to book two hotel rooms.

"Is this…Do you…" Words have failed me.

Her brow wrinkles and she surveys her outfit. "Is there a problem with what I'm wearing?"

Problem? No. Not at all. How she expects me to keep my hands off of her when she's wearing a satin tank top and matching shorts isn't a problem. At least not for her.

"Is this not how you expected me to dress for bed?" she asks when I continue to stand in front of her with my mouth hanging open. I hope I'm not drooling.

I clear my throat and force myself to concentrate on the conversation instead of on how my hands itch to touch her. "I did not have any expectations whatsoever about what you wear to sleep."

"Okay." She accepts my word without question, which is good because if I had to admit the truth – I imagined her wearing nothing to sleep – she'd skin me alive. "How did you know what to order for me?"

"Because I know you."

She places her hands on her hips causing the tank top to pull tight over her breasts and her nipples to press against the material. So much for concentrating on the conversation. I fist my hands to stop myself from reaching out and hauling her into my arms.

"What did you order me?"

"The vegetarian burger with no bun and grilled vegetables instead of fries."

She blinks in surprise, and her hands drop. "How did you know?"

"I told you. I know you," I say and flee to the bathroom before my body decides it wants to learn more about Lilac besides her preferred dinner choices. Things like what kind of noises she makes when I touch her naked breast and— I stop those thoughts. She needs to say yes first I remind myself.

"I'd prefer if you didn't jerk off in the shower," she shouts after me.

"I wasn't going to jerk off," I say with my hard cock in my hand.

"Well, I don't know how you're going to urinate with an erect penis. Of course, you could... Never mind. I promised my sisters no more talk about defecation."

At the word defecation, my cock deflates. I'm torn between relief and annoyance. I tuck it away and wash my hands before strolling back into the bedroom area.

"You were very quick."

I pretend to not know what she's talking about. "I forgot my clothes to change into," I lie before picking up my overnight bag and carrying it to the bathroom.

"I'm sorry if I embarrassed you. I can sit in the bar for fifteen minutes if you need quiet to handle your ...erm...needs."

Instead of explaining to her how she can help with any needs I have, I tell her, "I'll be out in a second. Our food should be here soon."

I quickly change into a pair of sweats and a t-shirt. When I exit the bathroom, there's a knock on the door to indicate the arrival of our food. I hurry to accept the food before Lilac can come to the door. I don't want anyone besides me to see her in her satin tank top.

Once I've arranged our food on the table, we sit down across from each other to eat. I tuck into my food but stop when I notice Lilac rubbing her arms.

"Are you cold?"

I don't wait for an answer and dig a sweatshirt out of my suitcase before handing it to her. "I'll turn down the air-conditioning, but in the meantime, wear this."

She sniffs the shirt before putting it on. Although she's mere inches shorter than me, she drowns in it. Male satisfaction blossoms in my chest at the sight of her wearing my clothes. If Lilac knew what I was thinking, she'd give me a lecture on men and their caveman tendencies. Since I've heard the lecture before, I settle back at the table and concentrate on my burger.

"Oh my," she says as she fans her face, "this vegetarian burger is a bit spicy."

"Is it too spicy? Do you want me to order you something else?"

"No, thank you. It's delicious. A bit spicier than I'm used to is all."

As I eat my burger, Lilac's face becomes redder and redder. A blush now runs from her cheeks down her neck. I can't help but wonder how much further it travels down her body.

She finishes her burger and downs her beer. She coughs as she sets the glass down. "Wow. It's warm in here now."

"Do you want me to switch the air-conditioning back on?"

"It's fine. I'll remove your sweatshirt."

She grasps the hem and whips the sweatshirt off of her. Except the sweatshirt isn't the only garment she removed. She also removed her tank top, leaving her completely topless in front of me, and answering my question as to how far her blush spreads.

I rush to grab the sweatshirt to cover her again, but I can't take my eyes off of her perfect body. Her blushing breasts are the perfect size for my hands. And, as I watch, her nipples pebble under my scrutiny. Shit. I shouldn't be gawking at her. I slam my eyes shut and drop to my knees on the floor to pat the area for my sweatshirt.

I find the garment and hold it out to her with my eyes still closed. I miss her hand and end up slapping the sweatshirt against her breast.

I drop my hand. "Shit. Sorry."

"I'm confused."

"About what?"

"Don't you want me?"

"Of course, I want you." I want to place her hand against my hard length to prove the truth of my words to her, but I know better. Instead, I squeeze it. "You can see how much I want you."

"I want you, too."

My eyes fly open, and I gaze up at her. "Are you sure?"

She scowls. "I hate when men question whether a woman knows what she wants. I know my own mind."

"I'm not questioning whether you know what you want. I'm questioning the change in direction. An hour ago, you told me I had to sleep on the floor."

She sighs. "I'm done fighting the chemistry between us. Maybe if we have sexual relations, it will burn through our chemistry."

I disagree. I've never experienced the kind of chemistry we have, but I'm convinced it can't be burned through in one night. And I don't want it to be. I want to enjoy our chemistry for as long as it lasts.

"I don't want there to be any misunderstanding. You're agreeing to have sexual intercourse with me tonight?"

She nods. "Only one time. And we won't speak of this afterwards. Especially not at work."

"No talk of sex at work," I agree, but I won't agree *not* to speak of it afterwards. We'll be doing a ton of speaking about it.

First things first. I wrap a hand around her ankle. "Last chance to change your mind."

"Have you ever known me to change my mind?"

I don't remind her she's changing her mind about having sex with me right now. I'm not a stupid man.

Chapter 16

Slow and steady – supposedly wins the race but no one is certain as to why

BECKETT

I run my hands up Lilac's silky smooth legs.

"You have the softest skin I've ever felt," I say as I watch goosebumps erupt on her skin.

"Thank you. I use a biological honey-based lotion. I can bring you a bottle of it if you want it."

I kiss the spot above her navel. "Is that why your skin always smells of honey?"

"I assume so. A human body doesn't usually produce a flower-like smell of its own accord."

I trace my fingers along the underside of her breasts. "If anyone could produce the smell, it'd be you."

She threads her fingers through my hair. "Are you going to talk all night or are we going to have sex?"

"What's your hurry? We have all night."

She presses my head down toward her center. "I'm not in a hurry. I'm impatient after you drove me crazy all day." She pushes on my head again.

I gaze up at her. "Is there something you want?"

"Yes," she huffs. "I want you to use your mouth on me."

I debate asking her where she wants me to use her mouth, but I have a feeling teasing won't work on Lilac.

"How's this?" I ask and place an open-mouthed kiss along the satin of her pajamas.

She growls in frustration. "Remove my shorts."

I bristle at the order. I prefer to be in charge in the bedroom, but I follow her order – sort of. I remove her satin shorts leaving her underwear on.

"How's this?" I ask as I run my finger along the elastic band of her panties.

She growls in frustration. "You deliberately misunderstood me."

I place a kiss against her inner thigh to hide my smile. I nibble at the skin for a while before hooking my thumbs in the waistband of her panties and drawing them down her legs until she's standing completely naked before me.

Finally. My cock jumps. He wants in her now. Too bad. He's going to have to wait because I'm on a mission. By the time my cock enters her, Lilac won't be giving me orders. No, she'll be too swept up in what she's feeling to remember to order me around.

"Open yourself to me. Put your leg on my shoulder."

She doesn't hesitate to follow my order and throws her leg over my shoulder. My mouth waters at the vision before me. My Lilac is finally where I want her to be. Ready to be pleasured by me.

I cup her ass checks and bring her center to my mouth. I latch onto her clit, and she moans. Her fingernails dig into my head and spur me on. While I suck on her, my fingers toy at her opening – not quite entering her.

Her moan becomes a growl. "Stop teasing me."

I hum and shove two fingers inside her. I'm done teasing. As much as I'm enjoying her taste in my mouth, my cock is heavy and aching to join in the action. I curl my fingers and massage her inner walls. She uses her hold on my hair to ride my fingers until she's moaning my name.

"Beckett!" she cries as her inner walls clench and she comes.

I slowly withdraw my fingers as her orgasm wanes. When her fingers unlatch from my hair, I pull away and place her foot back on the floor. Her legs tremble, and I hold onto her thighs until she's steady on her feet.

When I stand, I notice her face is flushed, her eyes are unfocused, and there's a line of sweat on her brow. She's never looked more beautiful. Her lips are tipped up in a barely there smile and I can't resist. I fist her hair and my lips crash onto hers. My tongue plunges into her mouth and she moans at the taste of herself.

I place my hands on her ass and lift until she gets the hint and hops into my arms. Her legs wrap around my waist, and I walk forward until I can press her against the glass window.

As I plunder her mouth, I thrust my covered cock into her center. She rubs herself against me until I feel pre-cum leaking out of the tip of my cock. I need to stop before I come in my pants like a damn teenager, but I can't seem to.

I use my hold on her ass to lift her up and down against my cock until she rips her mouth from mine and shouts, "Yes! Yes, Beckett."

I grit my teeth and count backward from one hundred as she comes again to stop myself from joining her. My balls draw up and my spine tingles, but she slows her movements before I can shoot off into my pants.

"That's two," I mutter when her gaze meets mine.

"Yes, I'm aware. And I can count."

"Can you count to three?"

Her brow wrinkles. "Of course, I can count to three."

I tweak her nose. "I was teasing."

"Oh."

"I meant do you want to try for three?"

"Do or do not. There is no try."

I freeze. "Did you just quote Yoda to me?"

She shrugs. "Star Wars is a good movie."

"Because Star Wars rocks." I kiss her nose. "Any other movie franchises you want to discuss before we begin the next portion of our evening?"

"It depends on what the next portion of the evening entails."

I bend over to whisper in her ear. "It involves me using my cock to make you come for a third time."

Goosebumps break out over her skin, and she shivers in my arms. "In that case, I'm amenable to moving forward and skipping a movie discussion."

"I thought you would be."

I whirl around and step toward the bed before dumping her on it. She bounces and her breasts jiggle as she giggles.

I pounce on her. "Are you laughing at me?"

She brushes the hair out of my face with a tender look on her face. With a start, I realize I want to see this look on her face every day for the rest of my life. I push those thoughts out of my mind. I have other things to concentrate on with a naked Lilac writhing beneath me.

"I would never laugh *at* you." She winks and my heart squeezes. There she is. The sweet woman I knew was hiding beneath the prickly exterior.

I pin her arms above her head and thrust my still clothed cock into her. She widens her legs and I settle my hips between them.

I thrust into her once again and she moans as her back arches. Her breasts jut out and I can't resist the temptation. I latch onto one and suck until the nipple is a hard pebble. Then, I switch to the other one.

Lilac squirms underneath me. "I thought we agreed on no teasing."

I nibble at her nipple with my teeth, and she groans. "I agreed to no such thing."

She pulls at the hold of my arms until I release her. As soon as her hands are free, she reaches for the hem of my shirt.

"You can't have a third act while you're clothed."

"You can't? Challenge accepted."

I bat her hands away from my t-shirt and push my sweats down just enough to free my cock. It bumps against her stom-

ach, and she's momentarily stunned. It's enough to allow me to shackle her wrists again.

I line my cock up with her opening. "You ready?"

She doesn't answer verbally. Instead, she pushes up until I enter her. Once my tip is inside her, she raises an eyebrow in challenge. I slam into her and we both groan.

I halt fully seated inside her. I can't move. If I do, this will be over before it began. Unacceptable.

"What's the matter?" Lilac asks as she squeezes her inner muscles around me. I groan and drop my forehead to hers.

"I don't want this to be quick, honey," I admit.

Confusion clouds her gaze. "There's nothing wrong with quick."

"But slow and gentle ain't bad either," I tell her as I withdraw inch by incredible inch before entering her again.

I keep my pace slow and steady with our foreheads touching and our gazes connected. More than our gazes are connected. We share more than white hot sexual chemistry. We have a connection – an undeniable connection.

I love Lilac I realize with a start. This smart, gorgeous, unbelievably complicated woman was made for me.

The realization that I have the woman I love beneath me causes my pace to quicken and she moans. I release her hands to reach down and rub her clit. Her legs tighten around my waist, and she squeezes me.

"I'm going to come," she gasps out as she stares into my eyes.

"Come," I order.

Her eyes fall shut and her neck arches back as her inner muscles spasm around me.

"Yes," I hiss as her orgasm triggers mine. "Yes," I mutter over and over again. "Lilac!" I cry when I finish.

I collapse on top of her before I remember to roll to her side before I crush her. I tuck her into my side.

"Sleep, honey. Sleep."

"I don't—"

"Just sleep," I cut her off before she can remind me of how she doesn't sleep with her lovers. I'm not one of her lovers. I'm the man who loves her.

My heart squeezes at the thought. Convincing Lilac to make love to me was one thing. Convincing her to give me a real chance is another.

And I thought things were complicated before. Welcome to the real complicated.

Chapter 17

Making love – a way to get yourself in deep, deep trouble

"ARGH!" Juniper screams. "Holy bats of Gotham."

I sigh as I watch my sister jolt before falling out of the window she's crawling through and collapsing on the floor.

"If I pee my pants, I'm killing you, Ashlyn."

"You can't kill me if you don't open the door," Ashlyn yells through my front door.

I grunt before standing and marching to the door to open it. Aspen and Ellery are standing there with Ashlyn. I should have known.

"What do you want?"

Ashlyn pushes her way past me. "To figure out why you're hiding."

I wait until everyone's inside and close the door after them. "I'm not hiding."

"Who cares if she's hiding? I'm dying here," Juniper complains as she rolls around on the floor.

"You're not dying. The electric shock you received is minimal." I'd explain how minimal, but my sisters always complain when I go into detail.

"You are so cool," Ashlyn gasps. "You wired your windows to give intruders an electric shock."

"No, I wired my window to give *you* an electric shock when *you* invade." One uninvited home invasion was my limit.

"Good thing Juniper led the charge today."

Juniper rolls until she's sitting up and leans her back against my sofa. Her face is gray and there are brackets of pain around her mouth. "This whole invasion was your idea. Not mine," she huffs.

"But I'm with baby." Ashlyn rubs her slightly rounded tummy.

"You won't be pregnant forever," Juniper grumbles. "I'll get my revenge eventually."

"What are you doing here?" I ask her. "Isn't Maverick home?"

Her brow wrinkles. "How do you know? I haven't told anyone he's home. It has to be those interfering gossip gals. Will they never leave me alone?"

"I didn't discuss Maverick's location with anyone. I set a Google alert for him."

"You're cyberstalking my boyfriend?"

"I'm not harassing or intimidating him."

Aspen claps her hands. "Can we get back to the matter at hand and talk about Lilac's computer skills later?"

"What is the matter at hand?" I ask because I know it annoys her when I say I don't understand what's happening. It's my strongest weapon against her.

"Why are you hiding from Beckett?"

"I'm not hiding." I omit the words 'from Beckett' to make the sentence true.

"Then, why are you working from home?" Ashlyn asks.

Ellery groans before collapsing on my sofa. "I wish I could work at home. No clients asking for extra towels. Extra towels they won't get, by the way. Do they not read the website before they make a reservation? I clearly indicate the bed and breakfast is ecologically responsible."

"Ecologically responsible is a vague term," I begin.

"Nope." Ashlyn thrusts her palm in my face. "No avoidance. Explain why you're working from home."

"How do you even know I'm working from home?"

"Duh. Cassandra told me."

I knew introducing Ashlyn to Beckett's sister was a bad idea.

"And how did Cassandra know?"

"Beckett told her you were avoiding him."

I feel panic bubbling up from inside of me until it explodes in the form of words bursting forth. "Why is Beckett talking to his sister about me? What else did he tell her? Is he telling everyone at the office we had sex? I'll lose my job."

"Hold up! Rewind. You had sex with Beckett! Whoo-hoo! High-five!" Ashlyn holds her palm up to me, but I ignore her. I don't give high-fives, and I certainly don't give high-fives about my sex life.

Aspen slaps her hand against Ashlyn's. "This is awesome. My job here is done."

"Does this mean I have to move?" Ellery asks from the sofa where she's now laying down. "I never realized how comfortable Lilac's couch is."

"Of course, we're not leaving. Lilac had sex with Beckett and now she's avoiding him. She needs our help," Juniper says.

Aspen rubs her hands together. "This is my favorite part."

"Your favorite part of what?"

She rolls her eyes. "The mating process, of course."

"The mating process? You make Lilac sound like a praying mantis luring Beckett in with her pheromones," Juniper says.

"Of course, she's not a praying mantis. She's not going to bite his head off," Aspen says.

"Not all males get their heads bit off. Some get away uninjured, although males do make up sixty percent of the female diet during mating season."

"Thank you, animal freak," Aspen says before turning to me. "What's wrong? Was Beckett not good in bed?"

"Rowan's awesome in bed. He does this thing with his tongue—"

Juniper groans. "Ugh! No, I don't want to hear about my baby sister and her husband having sex."

Ashlyn sticks her tongue out at her. "You're a few months older than me. I don't know why you insist on calling me the baby sister."

"I'm more than a year older than you. And you're the youngest, which is the very definition of baby sister."

"No, I'm the youngest of the family. I'm not a baby."

"Enough!" Ellery yells. "We're not here to discuss the proper terminology for the youngest child of the family."

"Someone's grumpy," Ashlyn sings.

"Someone hasn't had an uninterrupted night of sleep since Willow was born."

Ashlyn sighs. "I can't wait."

Aspen ignores Ashlyn and steps close to me. "What happened? Do you want to talk about it? Did he ask you to do things you're uncomfortable with?"

Does she think Beckett forced himself on me? Regardless of my feelings for the man, I can't allow her to have any misconceptions about him. "Beckett would never ask me to perform a sex act I'm uncomfortable with."

She throws her arms in the air. "I give up. I don't understand the problem."

"It's the boss thing," Ellery guesses.

Beckett being my boss is an issue, but it's not the primary issue at the moment. I consider how to answer. Do I continue to mislead my sisters, or do I confess to what the issue is?

"We might as well get comfortable," Ashlyn says as she settles into my recliner. "Lilac's not done giving us the runaround."

Aspen lifts Ellery's feet and makes herself comfortable on the sofa while Juniper sprawls on the floor.

I scan the room. "You're not going away until I tell you why I'm working at home?" A chorus of no's. "And you won't accept my need for privacy?"

Ashlyn snorts while my other sisters giggle at my question.

Based on their responses, misdirection will not work on them today.

"Fine. We didn't have sex."

"I'm confused." Ashlyn's nose scrunches. "Didn't she say they had sex less than five minutes ago?"

"Could he not finish?" Aspen asks. "Because it can happen with older men."

"Beckett is thirty-eight. He's not an 'older man'. And he finished just fine."

"Did he not get you off?" Juniper asks. "Sometimes you have to coach a man in what gets you off."

"I don't need to coach Rowan. He knows exactly what I enjoy in the bedroom. How hard. How soft. How much tongue."

I ignore Ashlyn. "The encounter was completely satisfactory to me."

"Just tell us!" Ellery demands. "The suspense is killing me."

I decide to give in as I do not have all night to discuss my sex life with my sisters.

"We didn't have sex. We made love."

Cheers erupt, and Ashlyn jumps to her feet and starts dancing.

"Yeah! I told you my work here is done," Aspen exclaims with her fist in the air.

Ellery pounds Aspen's fist. "This is awesome. I thought pairing off Lilac was asking for the impossible."

"Miracles happen," chimes Juniper.

"Enough!" I shout and everyone quiets down. Ashlyn stops dancing with her foot dangling in the air. "I am not in love, and I am not paired off. What I am is in trouble."

"What do you mean?" Aspen asks as she settles back on the sofa.

"Are you pregnant?" Ellery asks. "There's no shame in getting pregnant after a one-night stand."

I don't dignify her question with a response. "Did you forget Beckett is my boss? I can't make love to my boss."

"Agree to disagree," Ashlyn says as she resumes dancing. "It happens all the time."

"And how many of those women lose their jobs and ruin their careers?"

"I don't know. Should we do some research?" Juniper pulls out her phone and switches it on.

"My question was rhetorical."

"Shit," Ellery swears. "If Lilac's using rhetorical questions, we're in trouble."

Aspen places her hands on my shoulders. "But what if you don't lose your job? What if you fall in love and live happily ever after?"

"Statistically, the chance of falling in love and living happily ever after is unlikely."

"Who cares about statistics?"

Not care about statistics? Is Ashlyn crazy? Everyone should care about statistics. "I do."

Aspen squeezes my shoulders. "If Beckett made love to you, it means he thinks of you as more than a one-night stand."

"But we agreed. Only one time."

"Make a new agreement. An agreement to see where the relationship between you two can go."

"I told you. The relationship can go nowhere. He's my boss."

"How do these things work out in those books you narrate?" Aspen asks Ashlyn.

Ashlyn's nose scrunches. "Lots of drama happens, but it all works out in the end."

"I don't do drama."

"Too bad," Aspen says, "because you're in smack dab in the middle of drama now."

Which is exactly where I didn't want to be. I don't do complicated, and I don't do drama, both of which lead to confusing situations. I prefer to maintain relationships I know the boundaries of. A romantic relationship is not one of those.

"Think about it, Lilac," Juniper says as she climbs to her feet. "Don't you want a steady relationship like the ones we have?"

No, I don't think I do. People don't understand me. Beckett may think I'm fascinating now, but he'll grow frustrated with me the same way everyone else has. I can't risk it. I'd rather not try than fail in the end. I hate failing.

Chapter 18

Kidnapping – can sometimes end in the making of new friends

BECKETT

I load my groceries in the trunk and slam it shut before grabbing my shopping cart to return it. But when I begin to push the cart forward, four men move to block me. I don't recognize any of them, but guessing by the scowls on their faces, I've pissed them off.

"Can I help you?"

"You're coming with us," a man who's several inches taller and wider than me says.

"I am?" They don't appear threatening in their shorts and t-shirts with flip-flops, but I'm not in a hurry to go anywhere with them.

"Yep. It's about time we did another kidnapping," another man says.

The third man slaps him on the shoulder. "We didn't kidnap you." His words do not reassure me of their good intentions, despite the police uniform he's wearing.

"You did, but it's okay. It's payback time."

"I can't believe this is why you told me there was an emergency and I needed to return home immediately," the final man grumbles.

I narrow my eyes at him as he appears familiar, but it's hard to figure out how I may know him when his beard covers half of his face and the rest is in shadow from his ball cap.

"Come on," the one dressed in a police uniform says and waves a hand toward a car. I'm happy to see it's not a police car.

"Where are we going, officer?"

The big guy snorts. "Again with the officer. I swear you make us do these kidnappings to listen to people call you officer."

His words stop me cold. "Kidnappings?" As in plural? Are they serial kidnappers? Is there such a thing as a serial kidnapper? Too bad Lilac isn't here. She'd know. But the woman is avoiding me.

"Don't worry about it," the man who's slightly shorter than me says. "We won't harm you. Too much."

I glance around the parking lot, but no one's around. I'm not going to be a sissy and shout for help. At least not until I know what's happening here. I allow them to herd me into the car.

"What bar do you recommend?" the driver who appears familiar asks.

Bar? They're kidnapping me and taking me to a bar? And here I thought this encounter couldn't get any stranger.

"The White Stag?" Although it won't be crowded this early in the afternoon, it's on the main avenue through town. If I can get away from the men, I can make a break for freedom.

The officer clamps his hand down on my thigh. "Don't worry. There's no need to make a run for it."

I keep my mouth shut. I have no idea what's going on but talking my way out of this doesn't appear to be an option considering the police officer can read my mind.

We park on the street in front of the bar and climb out of the car. I glance up and down the street wondering if this is my chance to escape, but the officer wraps a hand around my bicep and motions to the door.

Inside the bar is dark. I frown as I scan the room. It's practically deserted, and the current patrons are not going to be of much help. Not when several of them appear to have passed out if their snoring is any indication.

I try to sit at a table near the window, but the big guy stops me before motioning toward a booth in the back. There goes my chance for signaling to a passerby. At least the booth in the back is near the rear hallway and emergency exit.

I take a seat and the big guy sits next to me. Crap. The only way I'm getting out of here without him moving is by crawling. Considering how my shoes are sticking to the floor, I don't think crawling is a viable option.

The man I'm convinced is in a disguise sits across from me and removes his beard and hat.

I gasp when his face is revealed. "Holy shit. You're Maverick Langston."

He grins as he shakes my hand. "Always happy to meet a fan."

"A fan?" The big guy next to me snorts. "He didn't say he was a fan. He said he knows who you are. Big deal."

I stare up at the giant. "Son of a bitch. You're Rowan Hansley."

He nods in acknowledgement.

"I didn't know you two were friends," I say as I glance between Rowan and Maverick.

Rowan chuckles. "More like family."

"Family?" I narrow my eyes and study the two of them, but I don't notice any family resemblance. "How does the world not know you're related?"

"I said we're family. I didn't say we're related."

Before I can puzzle out what he means, the officer returns and plunks a pitcher of beer down on the table as well as five glasses. "Are you done fawning over the actor and former football player?"

"Don't be jealous." Maverick winks at him.

"Never said I was jealous," he mutters as he pours me a beer and slides it across the table to me.

"I, for one, am glad we got another normie in our group," the fourth man says.

The officer laughs. "And you think you're normal? You didn't get Ellery pregnant during a one-night stand?"

He shrugs. "It happens. Besides, I wouldn't trade Willow for the world."

I clear my throat. "As much as I'm enjoying this conversation," I lie. "I'm not clear on why I'm here."

"Introduction time." The officer points to Maverick. "Maverick Langston, movie star and boyfriend of Juniper West." He points to Rowan. "Rowan Hansley, former NFL star, current bakery owner, and husband of Ashlyn West."

"And baby daddy," Rowan interrupts to add.

The officer ignores him and continues his introductions. "Cole Hawkins, fiancé of Ellery West and father of the first West grandchild."

"I'll show you some pictures of Willow," Cole – the same as every father before him – says.

"And I'm Lyric, Chief of Police of Winter Falls, and Aspen West's fiancé."

"West? You're Lilac's brothers-in-law?"

I remember Ashlyn saying something about her sister being engaged to Maverick Langston. I thought she was kidding. Guess not.

"Technically, I'm the only brother-in-law," Rowan says, and I recall Ashlyn pointing out the big guy as her husband at the Litha festival. I didn't pay any attention to the man at the time since I was too busy being caught up in Lilac. "The rest of them haven't managed to seal the deal yet."

"I got Aspen to set a date." Lyric lifts his glass, and the others cheer with him.

I sip on my beer as I observe the men over the rim of my glass. They appear completely calm, not as if they just committed a felony by kidnapping someone. I decide to take a chance.

"Why did you kidnap me?"

Cole snorts. "This isn't a kidnapping. I'm the only one who got kidnapped. The rest of you are a bunch of sissies who need to be coddled in a bar."

"It's not as if we tortured you," Lyric says.

"But you didn't buy me a beer either."

Maverick ignores Cole to explain, "This is your initiation into the West family."

I gulp. "Initiation?"

I pledged with a fraternity in college. Initiation brings back memories of running around the quad naked with my butt cheeks taped together. No matter how much you shave your butt beforehand, there's always hair the tape pulls away. Not to mention skin. I shiver. Never again.

Rowan slaps my shoulder. "No need to worry. We're not going to hurt you."

"Yeah. No one's going to dump a bucket of freezing cold water over you," Cole complains.

Lyric rolls his eyes. "Will you get over it already?"

"Maybe if you pay for this round of drinks."

Lyric snorts. "As if we ever pay anything when Maverick's around."

"Whoa!" Maverick holds up his hands. "Why are you bringing me into this? I wasn't around when you tried to drown Cole."

Lyric cocks his eyebrow. "You weren't?"

I look back and forth between the two of them. I have no idea what they're talking about, but I think it's safe to say they aren't really kidnapping me. Unless forcing me to drink a beer at four in the afternoon is considered kidnapping.

Maverick clears his throat. "Moving on. What are you doing with Lilac?"

My shoulders lose their tension. "This is the big brother intervention?"

"What else would it be?" Rowan pretends he doesn't know I had no idea who the four of them were when they pushed me into a car and drove me here.

"I have four younger sisters," I say. "I get it."

Cole moans. "Four younger sisters? I'm already stressing about having one daughter. I can't imagine having four."

"I raised them after our parents passed away before I turned nineteen."

"Shit," Cole swears. "We can't give him the third degree if he raised four girls when he was a teenager."

"We still need to ensure he won't mistreat Lilac." Lyric glares at me. "You may think Lilac doesn't have feelings because she appears all cool and collected, but she does, and they run deep. If you hurt her, she'll retreat into her shell, and we'll never get her out of it again."

"I know Lilac has feelings," I growl. "And I would never hurt her on purpose."

"Not 'on purpose' is the problem. Lilac's special. It's easy to hurt her on accident and we won't stand for it."

I glare at him as jealousy flares through me. "You seem to know a lot about her."

"I do. She's four years younger than me, but she was in several of my math and science classes while we were in high school since the woman's a genius. The other kids were not kind to her."

I grunt as relief fills me. Lyric and Lilac were obviously never involved. "Teenagers are assholes."

"But a man, a real man, would never be intimidated by a woman for being smarter than him."

I chuckle. "You think I don't know Lilac is smarter than me? I may be her boss, but half the time I don't understand what she's talking about."

"And it won't bother you if Lilac's more successful than you?" Cole asks. "If everyone in town refers to her and not you on matters."

"Hell. They better not refer to me on any environmental matters. I'm the CEO of the company, but I rely on my personnel for the day-to-day operations of the company."

"You do?" Maverick folds his arms across his chest and leans back against the seat. "You went with Lilac to the convention in San Francisco because you were relying on her for the day-to-day operations?"

I sigh. Somehow they know what happened in San Francisco. "Let's stop beating around the bush."

Lyric leans across the table. "Good idea. Let me make myself clear. If you cause Lilac to run and hide again, I will find you and I will gut you."

"And I'll help," Rowan adds.

"I don't actually know how to gut someone, but I'll alibi them," Cole claims.

"And I've got a private jet at my disposal," Maverick adds.

I gulp. "I understand."

"Now," Rowan says and stands, "who wants to play darts?"

He saunters off with the rest of them following as if they didn't just threaten to gut me.

They don't scare me, though. On the contrary, I'm glad Lilac has people watching out for her. In fact, I plan to be the main person watching out for her from now on. Just as soon as I can get her to stop avoiding me.

Chapter 19

Love – an illogical emotion that can sometimes be explained by logic

You got this!

Go Lilac!

Kick some ass!

Lilac! Lilac! Lilac!

I STARE AT THE messages on my phone. My sisters have been sending them all morning long.

Why are you pretending to be my personal cheerleaders?

Ashlyn: *Eyeroll emoji* Duh.

My baby sister doesn't understand the meaning of a clear statement.

Aspen: We want you to do well at work.

Me: I always do well at work.

Despite what Beckett may think about my capabilities, I am more than competent in my job. In fact, I excel in my field. I don't have to continue to work at *Clean Mountain Environment* since I receive job offers at least twice a month, but I choose to remain here.

> **Juniper: She means she wants you to do well at work *Wiggle eye emoji***

> **Me: You are all being confusing. I'm at work and switching my phone off.**

> **Ellery: They mean they want you to schlep the boss.**

> **Me: Only one time and our one time is over**

After I send my reminder to them of what my personal relationship with Beckett is, I switch my phone off.

"Knock. Knock," Brandi greets as she enters my office. "Beckett wanted you to know the meeting is starting in five minutes."

I check my watch. "The meeting time hasn't changed. Why did Beckett ask you to remind me?"

She shrugs. "Don't kill the messenger."

I stare at her retreating back. Why didn't Beckett come to remind me himself if he's worried I had forgotten? Or send me a message?

I pick up my phone and scroll through my messages searching for communications from Beckett, but I haven't received a single message from him since before our trip to San Francisco. This is most unusual.

Is Beckett finished with me? My stomach cramps at the thought. I know we agreed to only one time, and I may have claimed having sex with him once would burn through our chemistry, but it didn't. Not for me at least. He obviously feels otherwise if he's avoiding me.

My phone beeps to remind me of the meeting. I don't have time to examine my feelings on this situation now. I gather my things and make my way to the meeting room.

When I enter the room, I immediately move toward the open spot next to Beckett. When I try to pull the chair out, he grunts and points to an open spot on the opposite side of the room.

"What?" I don't understand. Whether I want to or not, as the lead environmental engineer in the company, I always sit next to Beckett in the monthly review meetings.

"This is Brandi's seat."

"Brandi doesn't attend these meetings."

The monthly review meeting is to discuss all of the ongoing engineering projects. There's no reason for Beckett's PA to attend.

"She does now."

"I'm here." Brandi pushes me out of the way and sits in the seat next to Beckett. She rolls the chair closer to him until they're practically touching.

I study the interaction for a moment until I realize what's happening. Beckett has replaced me with Brandi. Not on a professional level, of course. The woman is a horrible PA. She'd make an even worse engineer.

No, Beckett's moved on. I should have known. His obsession with me was fulfilled when we had sexual intercourse. I guess the chemistry I continue to feel is now one-sided. My stomach drops in disappointment.

I clench my teeth to stop myself from speaking as Brandi flips her hair and flutters her eyelashes at Beckett. Is she flirting with him? With a start, I realize I'm jealous. I don't want any other woman spending her time with him. And I definitely don't want anyone else to have sexual relations with him.

My mouth drops open as I realize I'm in love with Beckett. It's the only explanation that makes sense when I add up all the factors. I want to be the only woman in his life. I don't want him spending time with any other woman. I had sex with him without regard to using proper protection. I still feel this raw sexual chemistry with him. And, finally, I'm unable to control my emotional response when he's near.

I haven't experienced any of those emotions with another man. Only with Beckett. This is a most unexpected turn of events.

Jack snaps his fingers in front of my face. "Earth to Lilac. Earth to Lilac."

"Lilac's in her own world."

"I bet everything is black and white there."

I ignore the taunting. I've been dealing with bullies since I was twelve and attended math and science classes with high school seniors. Although Lyric tried to shield me from their teasing, he couldn't be around me all the time.

I thought the taunting would end when I was an adult working in a professional environment, but apparently, some people never grow out of the need to belittle others. According to my Sociology 101 class, bullying is a way for someone who feels inferior to feel superior.

Aspen can make fun of me all she wants for enrolling in those sociology classes. They've been eye-opening for me.

"Shall we begin," Beckett says, and I move to an open space on wooden legs and sit down. "Where are we at with Arkville?"

I open my file and outline the steps performed thus far.

"Arkville hasn't signed a contract with us yet?" Beckett asks once I've finished.

I frown. I just explained how the legal department is reviewing a few questions the city of Arkville has.

"As I said—"

Beckett cuts me off. "Brandi, make a note for me to contact the mayor."

I inhale a deep breath and let oxygen fill my lungs before blowing it out. I will not lose my temper with my boss at a meeting in front of the entire staff of engineers.

"I have a call with the mayor scheduled with the legal department today," I repeat information I already told him in my review.

Beckett waves my comment away. "Next up, Jack."

Did he dismiss me as if I don't matter? I understand he has no personal interest in me any longer – my stomach clenches at the thought – but dismissing me on a professional level is not okay.

I know he thinks I'm incompetent in my work – a matter I find puzzling since I'm the lead engineer – but outright dismissing me is just plain rude. Or so my sisters claim every time I supposedly 'dismiss' one of their inane arguments.

"Ahem," I clear my throat loudly before Jack, who's still digging around in his documents, can speak.

"I said I already have a call scheduled with the mayor of Arkville today. I don't think it's necessary for you to speak with him as well."

Beckett doesn't bother glancing up for his notepad where he's scribbling away. "I disagree."

"Oooh, burn." Jack does that juvenile thing where he licks his finger and then pretends it sizzles.

I slam my portfolio closed and stand. "If you'll excuse me, I need to…"

I let my words trail off as I march out of the room.

Once I'm standing in the hallway, I pause as I have no idea where to go or what to do. I've never lost control of my emotions and stormed out of a meeting before. I don't know what the protocol is for this situation.

My brow furrows as I realize this is the perfect excuse for Beckett to reprimand me. I've been trying to prove to him for a year now how I'm a competent engineer he can trust to get her work finished on time and in a satisfactory manner and I just ruined any progress I'd made.

Although, judging by his inability to allow me to manage the Arkville project, I hadn't made much progress in the past year anyway.

This is most unusual. I'm in love with a man who doesn't value my work. Perhaps my feelings are of lust and not love. The difference can be difficult to ascertain. Or, at least, those romance books Aspen makes me read each month indicate as much.

I need to research the matter. With my plan in place, I proceed to my office where I shut my door behind me ignoring Beckett's illogical open-door rule.

I pick up my phone to dial Aspen. My sisters will know how to proceed in this matter, but do I want to fill them in on my newly discovered feelings? I hesitate with my phone in my hand. They would most likely throw a party and declare themselves matchmaking queens of the world.

Their response would not be constructive whatsoever. I return my phone to my desk and wake my computer. It's better to conduct research on my own.

Chapter 20

Initiation – a ritual to gain acceptance in a family, often accompanied by menial tasks

BECKETT

I hesitate before I knock on the door of Mr. and Mrs. West. What if Lilac is here? What if she figures out I'm trying to bribe her mother into helping me? What if this whole thing is a set up?

It sounds plausible. Why else would Maverick message me and suggest I meet with Mrs. West to get her on my side? Immediately following his message, Lyric sent me a dispensation form to drive my car in Winter Falls, although I don't need a dispensation form since I drove my own electric car today.

This is crazy. I step back from the door intent on leaving when it opens.

"I thought you might chicken out," a woman says.

"Chicken out? Were you expecting me?" This whole thing *is* a setup.

"Not exactly."

Not exactly? What does 'not exactly' mean?

She holds out her hand. "I'm Ruby West. I'm Lilac's mother."

Aha! She was expecting me. Why else would she say she's Lilac's mother immediately upon meeting me?

I study her as we shake hands. Lilac doesn't resemble her in any way I can tell. She's short to Lilac's tall. She has blonde hair and blue eyes, whereas Lilac's hair is brown, and her eyes are the color of my favorite whiskey. She's also short and curvy. Lilac is tall and slender.

"Nice to meet you, Mrs. West."

"It's Ruby. Only the students at the high school refer to me as Mrs. West."

"Are you a teacher?" Lilac's mother is a teacher? I realize I know almost nothing about the family of the woman I love.

"I'm the principal." Her eyes twinkle with mischief. I bet she gives her students hell and enjoys every second of it.

"Come on." She steps onto the porch and shuts the door behind her.

"Where are we going?"

"Oh wait. I forgot." She whirls around and opens the door before grabbing a box. She hands me the box before shutting the door again.

"What's this?" I ask before I realize the box is full of packages of condoms. I want to throw the box back at her and run away, but I hold my ground. "Why are you giving me a box of condoms?"

"It's important to use prophylactics when having sexual intercourse."

I'm well aware of the need to use protection when having sex. I'm a thirty-eight-year-old man, not a teenager. Except when I think back on my night with Lilac, I realize we didn't use protection. Shit. Is Lilac pregnant? Is that why she ran out of the meeting yesterday?

No. It can't be. This is Lilac after all. She probably diagrams her monthly cycle.

Ruby pokes me in the chest. "Your look right now is why I insist on giving all of my girls' boyfriends condoms."

My look? I gulp. Can she tell I've had sex with her daughter and didn't protect her?

She rolls her eyes. "Of course, I know you've had sexual relations with my daughter."

"Can you read my mind?" I ask before I can think better of the question.

She giggles. "No, but the way you nearly swallowed your tongue when I said boyfriend and condoms in one sentence gave you away."

"You don't let the high school students get away with a thing, do you?"

"Nope." She winks.

"You're completely different than Lilac," I say before I can think better of it.

"Our Lilac's special." Damn right she is.

She studies me for a minute before reaching forward and squeezing my bicep. "I think you'll do."

Did she just give me her approval? She doesn't know anything about me.

"Now, put the box down. We have work to do."

"We do?"

I set the box on the table on the porch before following her around the house. She indicates a ladder leaning against the side.

"Do you want gloves? I think I have a pair in the shed."

Gloves? Why would I need gloves?

"The gutters can get clogged with dirt as well as twigs and other debris."

Does she mean for me to clean the gutters?

"I'll be back with some refreshments in an hour," she says and saunters away.

"Why am I cleaning your gutters?" I shout after her.

She rolls her eyes. "You can't expect my husband to do it. He's afraid of heights."

At least I didn't dress up to meet Mrs. West today. I remove my sweatshirt and climb the ladder to begin my assigned task.

I've barely begun to work when I hear a bottle opening. I look down to discover Lyric, Rowan, Cole, and Maverick sitting in chairs on the lawn. They've got a cooler between them and they're each holding a bottle of beer.

"What are you doing here?"

"Enjoying the show. Cheers!" Cole lifts his bottle in the air.

"Me cleaning gutters is the show?"

"It's not much of a show unless you take your shirt off," Maverick claims.

"Yeah, Becky Boy, why don't you take your shirt off?" I glance to the side and discover a group of elderly women dragging chairs across the lawn.

"Becky Boy?"

Lyric and Rowan jump to their feet to help the women. They set up the chairs and the women settle in them to apparently watch me clean gutters.

"I didn't realize Winter Falls was so boring, people got a kick out of watching someone clean gutters," I yell down to them.

"Oh please." One of the women rolls her eyes. "This isn't about you cleaning gutters."

"This is the West family initiation ritual," another woman says.

I swallow the lump that suddenly appears in my throat. Another initiation ritual. How many hoops do I have to jump through for Lilac? Not that I mind. She's worth jumping through all the hoops, although I do hope none of them are on fire. One incident with Cassandra and a match too close to my beard was enough for a lifetime.

Lyric points to the first woman to speak. "This is Sage. She's the police dispatcher and a pain in my ass."

The woman blows him an air kiss. "You couldn't live without me, and you know it."

He ignores her comment and continues with the introductions. "Sitting to her left is Feather. The other women are Petal, Cayenne, and Clove."

"Nice to meet you, ladies." I smile. "Sorry I can't shake your hands." I indicate my grimy hands.

"Oh, we don't want to shake your hand. We want you to remove your shirt," Feather says with a wiggle of her eyebrows.

"Take it off! Take it off!"

I turn to figure out who's shouting now. Ashlyn's cheering while pretending to have pompoms in her hands. Lilac's other sisters are behind her.

"Personally, I preferred it when you took your shirt off on the football field," a woman who must be Juniper as she's sitting on Maverick's lap says.

"You weren't there, June Bug."

"We recorded the entire thing for her," Ellery says as she hands a baby to Cole before sitting at his feet and leaning against his legs.

"Is someone recording this?" I ask as I scan the gathering crowd for someone holding their phone up.

Aspen waves her phone at me. "I am. I'm the official photographer."

"I thought you owned a bookstore." Didn't Lilac tell me her oldest sister ran a sexy book club at her bookstore?

"Are you going to talk all day or are you going to get those gutters cleaned?" Lyric asks.

"You have an awfully big mouth for someone who didn't have to do a West family initiation," Maverick mutters.

Lyric raises his eyebrow. "I didn't paint the outside of the high school?"

"I see you met the gossip gals." Ashlyn waves toward the group of elderly ladies.

"Um. Isn't it rude to say someone is a gossip?"

"We prefer the term busybody," Sage says.

"But then we realized gossip gal has a certain ring to it, don't you think?" Cayenne asks.

"I guess," I say, and they cheer.

Why didn't I keep my mouth shut? The women obviously aren't afraid to speak. They can defend themselves.

"Speaking of which, we should get gossip gal initiation day shirts made," Feather says.

"Lilac is the last West sister to get hitched," Ashlyn says. "It'd be a waste of a shirt."

"Silly girl," Sage tuts. "There are more single young people in town besides your family."

"You better not be talking about my brothers. Phoenix barely comes into town as it is. He's terrified you're going to try and matchmake him," Lyric says.

"Phoenix with the goats?" I ask.

"You met my brother?"

"Yes." And so did my sister. In fact, I think she has a bit of a crush on him since I caught her reading a book about goat farming the other day. Crap. This Phoenix guy doesn't appear interested in a relationship. Of course, the first man Gabrielle is interested in, in the past year, is relationship shy.

Ruby comes around the corner of the building and sighs when she notices the crowd. "I told you not to come by today."

"How are we going to figure out if he's good enough for our Lilac if we're not here for his West initiation?" Lyric asks.

"I'm just here to see him without his shirt on," Clove announces.

Ruby waves toward the street. "Go home and ask Sirius to remove his shirt if you want to see a man's naked chest."

Clove sighs. "I've seen his naked chest for thirty years. I'm entitled to a bit of variety."

"As for you lot," Ruby wags her finger at her daughters and their partners, "don't think I don't know you went to White Bridge to confront Beckett already."

"Does she have us chipped? How does she always know everything we do?" Rowan grumbles as he lifts Ashlyn off of his lap and stands.

Ashlyn raises her hand. "I didn't go to White Bridge."

"Beckett will be at Sunday family dinner tomorrow. You can harass him then."

Harass me? This isn't enough harassment?

Ruby glances up at me and winks. "Don't worry. I got your back."

I hope to hell so, because it appears I have another loop to jump through tomorrow.

Chapter 21

Interpretation – an explanation that differs based on whether you're sitting at the table or haven't entered the room yet

I ENTER MY PARENTS' house on Sunday afternoon for our weekly Sunday dinner to discover everyone except my father is here already. I check my watch and realize I'm five minutes earlier than normal. Why is everyone here ahead of me? And why is everyone's attention glued to the door?

"Why is everyone on time today?"

Ashlyn widens her eyes. "No reason."

I cock an eyebrow at her. If the widened eyes hadn't already given her away, her answer of 'no reason' would. She's obviously plotting something.

Everyone thinks I'm oblivious to the scheming my sisters and the rest of Winter Falls do. I'm not. I simply choose to not be involved. I have more important things to do with my time than bet on the gender of Ashlyn's baby or whether Forest will arrive at the monthly meeting wearing pants, although I do prefer it when he's clothed.

There's a knock on the door and I move to answer it as I'm the closest but Aspen tackles me to the floor before I can get there. I shove her off of me and stand.

"What are you doing? What is wrong with you? This is not a football field."

"Welcome," Mom greets the person at the door.

"Thanks for inviting me, Ruby."

I shiver at the sound of Beckett's voice and my feet automatically carry me toward him, but then I remember how distant he's been acting ever since we had sex and force my feet to stop moving. I may have realized I love the man, but I am not going to throw myself at him. He has already proven how quickly he grew tired of me.

"Why is my boss here? And why is he calling Mom Ruby?"

"I asked him to call me Ruby," Mom says as she carries a bundle of flowers to the kitchen.

"Someone's a suck up," Rowan mutters under his breath.

"Cleaning her gutters wasn't enough?" Cole grumbles.

I'm confused. "Is cleaning gutters a euphemism?"

Ashlyn giggles. "You don't honestly think Beckett and Mom—" Her words cut off as she swallows and places a hand on her stomach. "Thanks for the visual, Lilac."

"Must you insist on pretending to be squeamish about our parents' sex life?" I can't resist asking.

She pretends to gag, and I glance away before she notices my humor.

"Hello, Lilac," Beckett greets as he joins us in the living room.

"Hello," I respond because Mom doesn't allow rudeness in her house. "What are you doing here?" This question is based on curiosity and is therefore not rude.

"He's your paramour. Of course, he's here." Ashlyn waggles her eyebrows.

"How many times do I have to explain to you paramour refers to an illicit affair?"

Ashlyn shrugs. "Until I stop finding it amusing?"

"I invited him," Mom says as she returns with the flowers in a jug and places them on the table.

"Why?"

"Because you're involved."

"We're not involved."

"You had sex with him."

I don't bother asking Mom how she knows we had sex. It's impossible to keep a secret from my mother. I don't know how she manages it, but she knows more about what's going on in town than the gossip gals, which is saying a lot. At least she's more discreet than the gossip gals. Or, I should say, she usually is.

"I did, but it was a mistake."

"It wasn't a mistake," Beckett growls.

My stomach tingles at his growl, but I ignore it the same way he's ignored me for the past week at work. "I thought you understood it was a mistake. Why else have you been unfriendly to me at work?"

"I haven't been unfriendly to you at work."

"Yes, you have. Do you need examples?" I don't wait for his answer before beginning, "You had Brandi sit next to you at the monthly meeting and you flirted with her."

"I didn't flirt with her."

Lyric snarls. "You flirted with another woman in front of Lilac?"

Beckett holds up his palms. "I was trying to follow the rules Lilac set up."

"I set up?" Is he seriously blaming me for his flirting with another woman? "I didn't set up a rule about you flirting with your PA during meetings in front of the entire engineering staff."

"I wasn't flirting."

I ignore him. I'm not an idiot. I may be socially inept and awkward, but I know when two people are flirting.

"In addition to flirting with another woman, you berated me because I haven't managed to close the deal with Arkville yet."

"I didn't berate you."

"You insisted on contacting the mayor despite knowing I had a call scheduled with him to discuss the contractual terms."

"I wasn't—"

"Dude," Rowan interrupts, "you're never going to win an argument with her. You might as well give up now."

"I'm never giving up."

"Okay, I can detail further ways in which you've been un-friendly and unsympathetic or aloof to me at work." I fish my phone out of my pocket. "On Thursday, you—"

Beckett snatches my phone from me. "I didn't mean you should list every interaction we've had at work for your entire family."

I hold out my hand for my phone. "How else do you expect me to prove you've been unfriendly to me at work?" He frowns at my hand but after a brief hesitation lays my phone in it.

"I've heard enough," Lyric grumbles. "Your provisional approval has been withdrawn."

Provisional approval? "What are you talking about?"

"Now, now. There's no need to be hasty," Mom interjects. "Maybe he flirted with his PA to make Lilac jealous?"

Ashlyn giggles. "Bad idea, dude. Bad idea."

Beckett's hands fist at his hips. "I didn't flirt with Brandi."

"Oh boy." Ellery rolls her eyes. "Please tell me her name isn't Brandi with an i."

"I'm unsure how the spelling of his PA's name is relevant to this conversation."

She sighs. "It's with an i."

Cole wraps an arm around her and peers down at Willow who's laying in her mother's arms. "Your daddy knows better than to flirt with another woman no matter how her name is spelled."

"Does no one want to listen to my side of the story?" Beckett asks.

"Sorry. Not sorry. This one." Aspen points to me. "Doesn't lie."

"What if she misunderstood what she saw?"

"It's possible." Aspen taps her chin before asking me, "What did you see, Lilac?"

"Brandi pushed her chair as close to Beckett's as possible. She then tossed her hair and fluttered her eyelashes at him."

Juniper pokes Maverick. "I hope you know I'd kill you if you let your PA act that way."

Maverick nuzzles her neck. "I learned my lesson, June Bug."

"What about how I responded?" Beckett asks the crowd.

"This ought to be good," Ashlyn mutters. "How did you respond?"

"He smiled at her," I answer before he can.

"Boo!" Ashlyn and Juniper shout together.

Ellery glares at them. "You're lucky Willow's not sleeping."

"I smiled at her while I asked her to scoot her chair away from me," Beckett explains.

I cross my arms over my chest. This relationship stuff is confusing. Why would you smile at someone when you're unhappy with what they're doing?

"But she didn't move her chair."

He throws his arms in the air. "What did you want me to do? Yell at her in front of everyone."

"I don't know why not. You had no problem indicating your disapproval of my handling of the Arkville contract in front of everyone. Why is yelling at Brandi in front of everyone any different?"

I'm not asking a rhetorical question. I'm genuinely confused why Brandi received special treatment and I did not.

"I didn't want to embarrass her. Plus, I didn't yell at you in front of everyone."

"But you made it clear – once again – how you believe me to be incompetent."

"I don't …" He sighs. "Maybe I should leave."

"Good idea. Mixing business and personal life is a bad idea."

"I'm not leaving because whatever is happening between us is over."

"But it is over. We agreed. Only one time."

He growls. "I never agreed to your terms."

"Your agreement was implicit in carrying forth with our sexual encounter after I made my terms explicit."

"Someone stop her! She's talking about sex like it's a contract," Ashlyn grumbles.

"Dream girl," Rowan warns.

"You're right," Beckett says. "I should not have had sex with you knowing you thought it would be a one time thing when I planned to convince you for more."

He wants more? I want more. But wait. I can't have more. He's still my boss. My boss who flirted with another woman in my presence during a business meeting.

"You thought by being aloof at work I would be convinced to have sex with you again?"

He shrugs.

"What about calling me incompetent? Did you think I'd find you sexually attractive when you questioned my skill level?"

He runs a hand through his hair before tugging on the ends. "Maybe I should leave," he repeats.

I cross my arms over my chest and glare at him. "Yes, I think that is a good idea."

He kisses Mom goodbye before striding out the door. I asked him to leave, so I can't feel upset at his following my request. Yet, I do.

This is exactly why I didn't want to get involved with him. I knew any involvement would be complicated. I was right. For the first time in my life, I'm not enjoying being proven right. In fact, I'm quite certain I wouldn't mind being proven incorrect in this instance.

Chapter 22

Precise – ensuring details are correct to the point of annoying every other person in the room

BECKETT

I walk into the bar named *Electric Vibes*. If I weren't in Winter Falls, I'd assume I was in the wrong place. A hippie bar with every type of paraphernalia from the height of the hippie revolution you can think of displayed in every nook and cranny is not where I would expect a monthly pub quiz to normally happen.

But there's nothing 'normal' about Winter Falls. I'm discovering I enjoy the quirky little town. Which is a good thing since I know Lilac is committed to staying in the area. And I have no plans to give up on her, which is why I'm here this evening.

Ashlyn waves from a table in the middle of the room. I start to make my way there but am stopped by someone who appears to be the reincarnation of John Lennon.

"Holy shit," I mumble as I notice his round glasses, shaggy shoulder-length hair, and scraggly beard.

"Nothing holy about my shit," he mutters. "What team are you on?"

"I'm with the West sisters."

He glances up from his clipboard. "You're Lilac's man?"

"Um…" I want to be, but since she kicked me out of her parents' house on Sunday, I don't think I have the right to refer to myself as her man. In fact, I think she'd give me a lecture about women's equality if I dared to say I was her man.

"What's the holdup?"

I turn around to discover the elderly women who watched me clean the gutters at the West house standing behind me.

"Hello," I greet.

"I have ten dollars on Lilac walking out," Sage says in response.

"No way," Feather argues. "I have twenty dollars on the West sisters winning the quiz."

"You can't bet on them winning," Sage claims. "They always win, unless Lilac isn't here."

"Is Lilac coming tonight?" Feather asks.

Cayenne pokes me in the chest. "She's asking you."

"Um…"

Ashlyn wraps her hand around my bicep. "Leave him alone."

"Leave him alone? Why would we leave him alone? Have you met us?"

"Of course, I've met you, Sage. You brag about changing my diapers all the time," Ashlyn says before dragging me to a table in the middle of the room where Juniper and Aspen are already seated.

"You need to avoid the gossip gals while you're in the courting stage," Ashlyn explains as we sit down.

"Where's Lilac?" I ask since I already plan to avoid the elderly ladies and their scheming. Plus, I have no intention of discussing my courting Lilac with her sisters.

"We're giving you the benefit of the doubt here," Aspen says instead of answering my question.

"Yeah," Juniper agrees. "But if we discover you've been flirting with another woman again." She draws her index finger slowly across her neck.

"I have glitter bombs and I know how to use them," Ashlyn sings.

Damn it. I don't want to explain to Lilac's sisters how I was flirting with Brandi to get a rise out of Lilac. I know it was wrong and immature and I shouldn't have done it. But I need to apologize to Lilac before I explain my reasoning to any of them.

Lilac arrives, but she doesn't sit down. She glares at me instead. "What is he doing here?"

"He's filling in for Ellery. She has Willow tonight since Cole has to work," Ashlyn says with a bat of her eyelashes.

Lilac glares at her sister. "One, I'm working with Cole on the community center project and know he doesn't need to work tonight. Two, we don't need someone to fill in for Ellery. We're perfectly capable of winning the quiz without her."

"What about sports questions?" Juniper asks.

Lilac huffs. "Ashlyn is our expert in sports. You're our expert in all things related to animals and nature. And Aspen's our expert in literature."

"I'm quite good in geography and business questions," I say. "I—

"He's already signed in," Aspen cuts her off to say.

"Fine." Lilac grabs a chair from the table behind her and attempts to slide it in between Juniper and Aspen's chairs, but they refuse to make room for her.

"There's an empty chair here." Ashlyn points to the chair between the two of us.

Lilac flings the chair behind her, and it slams into a man.

"Who had Lilac hitting someone with a chair?" Sage shouts from her table beside the stage.

"I did!" Ashlyn yells and lifts her arms in victory.

"I'm sorry, Forest," Lilac apologizes. "I behaved inappropriately, and my careless actions ended up with you hurt. Can I buy you a beverage in apology?"

She shifts her weight from side to side as heat creeps up her face. Fuck. I want to insinuate my way into her life, but I don't want to embarrass her. I've been embarrassing her enough at work with how I've been behaving.

I stand, intent on leaving when I notice the man is wearing the smallest pair of Speedos I've ever seen.

"Why are you wearing Speedos?" I ask.

"Because we told him he couldn't swing his dick in the breeze during the pub quiz," Ashlyn answers on his behalf.

I choke on air and end up coughing. "What?"

"Tourists sometimes come to these events," Lilac explains.

I'm still confused. "And the Speedos are for the tourists?"

"Forest is a nudist," Juniper responds.

"Technically, he's not," Lilac corrects and Forest glowers at her. "It's true. A nudist is a person who enjoys being entirely nude. You enjoy not wearing pants."

"If everyone could take their seats, it's time to get started," the John Lennon-lookalike who checked me in says from the stage.

Lilac plops down in the chair next to me, and I decide to stick this thing out. She'll calm down eventually. I hope.

"Betting is now closed," Sage announces from her corner.

"Betting? What is everyone betting about?" I ask.

"Those women are the gossip gals." She indicates the table where the elderly women are sitting.

I don't tell her I met the women while I was cleaning out the gutters at her parents' house. She was mad enough when I showed up at their house for Sunday dinner. She'll lose her mind if she knows I was sucking up to her mom.

"And that's Lennon," she points to the MC.

"Lennon? As in John Lennon?" I can't deny the name fits.

"Yes. He's a bit obsessed with the former member of the Beatles."

"Usual rules apply," Lennon says. "The first person to raise their hand will be called on for the answer. If the answer is correct, we'll move on to the next question. If the answer is incorrect, the second person to have raised their hand will be asked to answer the question. And so on."

Ashlyn pours glasses of beer and hands them to Lilac, Aspen, and Juniper. "Usual rules apply. You have to chug the beer whenever you or anyone else on the team get the answer wrong. Or whenever anyone else in the pub gets the answer correct."

"This is ridiculous. This is your rule and yet you can't drink."

Ashlyn winks at Lilac. "And yet, the rule lives on."

"Why doesn't Beckett have a glass?"

"He's driving. Unless," she pauses with the pitcher poised over another glass, "he's spending the night at your house?"

I would love to spend the night at Lilac's house in her bed, but I'm not surprised when she mutters, "He is not." I know I have a lot of work to do before I'm welcome back in her bed.

"The first question is …" Lennon pauses until the crowd quiets down. "Who lives at 221B Baker Street?"

Someone shouts out Sherlock Holmes.

"Correct," Lennon nods in their direction.

"Drink," Ashlyn shouts at her sisters.

"No," Aspen refuses before hollering, "No one lives at 221B Baker Street as it doesn't exist!"

"Technically, it's now a museum," Lilac adds.

Aspen glares at her. "Do people live at museums?"

"Point is granted to the Sisters of Mayhem."

"We're the Sisters of Mayhem," Ashlyn explains with a smirk on her face.

"She's very proud of her ability to cause mayhem," Lilac whispers to me.

"Hey! If you've got it, flaunt it." Ashlyn winks.

"Next question," Lennon shouts. "Which Greek hero performed the twelve labors?"

Lilac raises her hand and waits for him to nod in her direction. "Heracles."

"Beep. Incorrect. Hercules."

A hush falls over the crowd and everyone's attention focuses on Lilac who raises her hand again.

Lennon sighs. "Yes, Lilac?"

"You said Greek hero. Hercules is the Latin name. Heracles is the Greek name."

"Fact checker!"

Forest climbs onto the stage in his tiny speedos and nothing else having now ditched his t-shirt and shoes. "Google says Lilac is correct."

Lilac bristles. "As if you need Google to check my information."

I squeeze her thigh and she inhales a quick breath. "Good job," I whisper and enjoy watching goosebumps break out on her skin.

"Next question. Who was the first man to circumnavigate the globe?"

"Ferdinand Magellan," someone yells.

I raise my hand and wait for Lennon to call on me.

"Ferdinand Magellan never circumnavigated the globe. He died halfway through the voyage. Juan Sebastian Elcano is the correct answer."

"He is correct," Lilac says.

"Another point for the Sisters of Mayhem."

I lean over and whisper in Lilac's ear, "Thanks for having my back, honey."

She shivers and a blush spreads from her cheeks down her neck. And I decide I don't care what I have to do to win Lilac back. Will it be difficult? Damn right, it will. But will it be worth it? Hell yeah, it will.

Chapter 23

Take a chance — do something you find scary as hell, but the alternative is worse, so you decide to go with scary

Beckett holds the passenger door of his car open for me and raises a brow toward me in challenge.

"I do not need you to drive me home," I say. "I have my bike here." I motion to my bike leaning against the side of the bar.

"But you've been drinking," Ashlyn shouts from the back seat. "Remember the time you got drunk and fell off your bike and broke your arm?"

"That was you. Not me."

Ashlyn giggles. "Right you are."

"Besides, I limited my alcohol intake to one glass of beer."

Ashlyn grunts. "I think we need to change the rules. You have to chug a beer every time you get the answer correct. Ms. Smarty Pants here never gets the answers wrong."

Beckett sighs. "Will you please get in the car so I can drive Ashlyn home? I promised Rowan I'd have her home safe immediately after the quiz."

"Rowan doesn't run my life. I'm an independent woman!" Ashlyn punches her fist into the air, and it slams into the roof of the car. "Ow. Your car hurt me, Beckett."

"You know she's going to continue saying crazy shit until you get in the car."

"You could drive her home without me."

His jaw clenches. "Not happening."

"What about my bike?"

Ashlyn snorts. "You can't seriously be worried someone's going to steal your bike. Did you forget we live in Winter Falls?"

"I got it." Juniper straddles her bike before grasping the handlebars of mine and pedaling away. "I'll drop it off at your apartment."

"Someone's out of excuses," Ashlyn sings from the back seat.

"I can walk."

"Ten bucks says she walks home," Sage hollers.

"I'll take your bet and raise you ten. I bet Beckett brings her home and stays the night," Feather responds.

I groan before getting into the car. "Stupid betting in this town. It should be illegal."

"You tried to ban it, remember? You almost got ran out of town with pitchforks."

"There were no pitchforks involved," I correct, because getting the facts correct is important.

"But you admit you almost got ran out of town."

Beckett sits in the driver seat and switches on the engine. "Where to, Ashlyn?"

"You can drop me off first," I tell him.

"My house is on the way to your apartment," Ashlyn says.

Beckett raises an eyebrow at me, and I answer truthfully, "She is correct."

We drive the three blocks to Rowan and Ashlyn's home. Rowan is standing on the porch waiting for us with his arms crossed over his chest.

"Oh goodie, I hope I'm in trouble," Ashlyn says as she bounces out of the car and up the driveway. When she reaches the porch, she launches herself at her husband. He catches her and carries her inside while waving to us.

"Take a left at the end of this street," I tell Beckett once we're driving again.

"I know where to drive."

"You do? How do you know where I live?"

"It's in your personnel file."

Oh, of course.

We arrive at my apartment mere moments later. Winter Falls is a small town with a mere 1,001 residents after all.

"Thank you for the ride," I say to Beckett, but he's already out of the car and rounding the hood. When he opens the door, I tell him, "You didn't need to open my door. I'm perfectly capable of opening my own door."

He grasps my hand and helps me out of the car. "I know you're capable. Lilac Bean West can do anything she puts her mind to. But there's nothing wrong with my being a gentleman."

I think on his answer for a few moments. "You are correct. You being a gentleman and my being an independent woman are not mutually exclusive."

He places a hand on my lower back as he accompanies me to the entrance of my building. His hand caresses my hip as we walk, and I lean into him. By the time we reach the door, our bodies are touching and my center is tingling.

"I don't think we should have sex," I blurt out.

"I wasn't offering."

While I contemplate why he's rejecting me, he snatches the keys from my hand and opens the door. He motions me inside and we climb the stairs to my apartment.

"Why are you following me if you don't want sex?"

"I want to talk."

I raise an eyebrow. "Talk about what?"

"Let's get inside your apartment before we continue."

I contemplate him a moment. Do I want to talk to him? If it's about work, it can wait. And, if it's not about work, I'm unsure as to how to proceed. Although, I am curious as to what he wants to discuss and there's only one way to find out. I nod my agreement. He opens the door and returns my keys to me.

"We're inside. You may continue."

He chuckles. "Can we sit down or are we going to have the most important conversation of my life in the hallway?"

"The most important conversation of your life? I didn't realize you were prone to exaggeration."

"I'm not." He taps my nose. "Shall we sit down?"

I sigh before leading him to my living room. His gaze studies the interior as he makes his way to the sofa and sits. I sit on the edge of the recliner, which is as far from him as I can be while still staying in the same room. My fingers drum on my thighs while I wait for him to speak.

"I was flirting with Brandi."

My stomach churns and my heart clenches at his admission. I've never been a jealous person before, but when it comes to Beckett my normal reactions don't apply, which is one of the reasons I'm convinced my feelings for him are love.

"Yes, I'm aware."

"I did it to make you jealous."

I'm not often at a loss for words, but I find myself at a loss now. "What? Why?"

"Because you act as if our night together meant nothing."

"We agreed we would have sex only one time. I'm confused as to how you expected me to act."

"I expected you to realize there's more to us than a night of sex."

My brows knit in confusion. "More to us?"

"Damnit, Lilac," he growls, "I love you."

He loves me? This doesn't make sense. He hasn't acted like a man in love. I've observed my parents and their loving relationship my entire life. And over the past year, I've stood by as one sister after another has fallen in love. I know how loving couples are with each other. It all starts with respect.

"You can't love me. You think I'm incompetent at my work."

"I don't think you're incompetent," he grumbles.

"I disagree. You constantly question me. You show up at meetings when you're not needed as if I can't handle the meeting myself. You turn up on site to check I'm not making errors."

"I admit I did those things."

"There's no reason for you to admit your behavior. I know it happened."

He sighs. "Can I explain?"

I motion for him to continue.

"I kept showing up at meetings and on site because I can't stay away from you."

This is most irregular. "You made me feel incompetent because you can't stay away from me?"

He runs a hand through his hair. "I never meant to make you feel incompetent. Watching you work – especially when you told the supervisor off at the biomass plant – is a sight to behold. You're the smartest person I know and you're not afraid to show it."

My brow furrows. "Why would I be afraid to show I'm intelligent?"

He grins. "Never mind."

He kneels in front of me and places his hands on my thighs. "Lilac, I'm madly in love with you. Will you take a chance on me?"

He may love me, but he's still my boss. "What about our work situation?"

"We can keep our relationship at work a secret."

"Keeping a secret is the same as lying and I prefer not to lie."

He grasps my hands. "You don't have to lie. You just have to not tell anyone we're involved."

"Omitting information is the same as a lie."

He squeezes my hands. "Do you have another suggestion?"

"There's only one other option. We don't proceed with a relationship."

His eyes close and his chin dips. "Is that what you want?"

I can't lie. Or, rather, I prefer not to lie. Misunderstandings are the result of lying. Thus, my belief Beckett thought I was incompetent.

"No." He smiles. "But I think it's for the best."

His smile dies, but his jaw clenches with determination. "Why do you prefer not to lie?"

"It's wrong."

"Yes, and?" he prods.

"It can lead to misunderstandings and conflict causing hurt. In the worst case scenario, lies lead to war."

"Okay. Now, tell me. Who will be hurt by us not telling the office about our relationship?"

I open my mouth to quote the office policy regarding inter-office relationships but close it just as quickly when I realize it's not applicable here. The person who can be hurt in this situation isn't just anyone at the office. It's me.

I gaze into Beckett's blue eyes with those flecks of gray as I debate with myself. Do I let the man I love go because I'm afraid? Or, do I take a chance? And hope he doesn't hurt me? What about if he tires of me or my awkwardness? I'll be heartbroken if he leaves me.

And the alternative? Letting him go and being forced to witness him move on to someone else? Brandi perhaps? No. I can't let that happen. I need to at least give the man a chance. Besides, I love him. A fact I don't plan on informing him of. At least not yet.

"Okay."

He cradles my face with my hands. "Are you saying what I think you're saying?"

"It depends. What do you think I'm saying?"

He grins. "You want to be with me."

I nod. "You are correct in your assessment."

He leans his forehead against mine. "Thank you."

"For what?"

"For taking a chance on me. I know this isn't easy for you. I know you worry about the effect being with me will have on your career."

He pushes to his feet before reaching down to lift me in his arms. "Which way is the bedroom?"

"I thought you didn't want to have sex."

He chuckles. "Honey, I want to have sex with you all the time."

"No sex at work," I declare. "We need to have boundaries."

"What about kissing?"

He doesn't wait for me to answer before his mouth crashes down upon mine. I moan at the feel of his lips and his tongue immediately seeks entrance. I thread my hands through his hair to bring him closer to me as our tongues duel for supremacy. Our teeth clash and I wrap my legs around his hips.

He yanks his mouth away. "Unless you want me to have sex with you against the wall, you need to stop grinding against me."

At his proclamation, I still my movements. "What's wrong with sex against the wall?"

He smirks. "I love your wild side, but I need a bed if I'm going to kiss every inch of your body."

Kiss every inch of my body? This is not a question I need to analyze.

I gesture toward the second door off the hallway. "The bedroom's through there."

Chapter 24

Normal – an idea perpetuated by boring people who are afraid of being different

THE ALARM CLOCK BLARES, and I sigh and snuggle into my pillow promising myself I'll get out of bed in just a minute. My pillow chuckles before wrapping an arm around my middle. My eyes fly open. How did I forget Beckett's in bed with me? And how is sleeping with him this comfortable?

Until the night in our hotel room in San Francisco, I'd never slept with a man before. I need my space at night. I don't want anyone crowding me. But Beckett is currently curled around me leaving me no space and I'm perfectly comfortable.

This must be another indication I'm in love with him. I couldn't fathom any other man crowding me in this way and not elbowing him in the ribs before kicking him out of my bed.

"Turn off the alarm, honey," Beckett mumbles into my ear before nibbling on the lobe.

"I can't," I protest even as I squirm in his arms.

His hand on my stomach moves to my naked breast and he massages it. "You sure? It's Saturday."

He plucks at my nipple, and I groan as I thrust my chest into his hand. His other hand joins the first and he kneads and molds my breasts while I grind my backside into his hard length. He thrusts against me before one hand abandons my breast to pull my panties down.

Bang! Bang! Bang!

I freeze at the sound of the neighbor pounding on our shared wall. I realize my alarm is now blaring and it's 9 a.m. on a Saturday morning. I push Beckett's hands away and crawl out of bed to switch off my alarm.

He groans. "Why is your alarm set for o' dark thirty on a Saturday morning anyway?"

"I don't know what time o' dark thirty is, but I have an engagement this morning."

He props his head on his elbow as he watches me remove clothes from my chest of drawers. "What engagement?"

"My sister's book launch."

"Your sister wrote a book? Which one?" He jumps out of bed. "I'll join you in the shower. Then, we won't be late."

"*We* won't be late? I don't recall inviting you."

"This is what couples do. They spend their weekends together."

I'm still contemplating whether his statement is true when he nabs my hand and drags me into the bathroom.

He winks at me. "And shower sex is awesome."

Forty-five minutes later, I sigh at Beckett as he reaches up to rub his eye again. I pull his hand away and maintain my hold on it as we walk toward Main Street.

"Stop it. You're making it worse."

"It stings," he complains.

"You're the one who claimed shower sex is awesome."

"Yeah well, I didn't expect your bottle of shampoo to attack me."

I shrug. "I warned you not to move."

"I thought you didn't want me to move because you were close."

I cock an eyebrow. "I guess you learned not to tease me during coitus."

He barks out a laugh. "Honey, the only thing I learned is your shampoo is aggressive."

I frown. "It shouldn't be. It's all-natural."

"Apparently, all-natural doesn't mean it won't sting like hell when poured directly into your eye."

"To be fair, I don't think Soleil considered our particular situation when she made the shampoo."

"Who's Soleil?"

"A local tradeswoman. She makes natural honey products, does pottery, and knits vibrator covers, among other things."

He stares at me with his mouth gaping open. "Did you say knits vibrator covers?"

"Yes. Apparently, they're quite popular."

He chuckles. "You never did tell me which sister wrote a book and what it's about."

"Actually, it's two of my sisters – Ashlyn and Aspen. The book details their treasure hunt."

His eyes widen. "Treasure hunt? I'm intrigued."

"It all began when Aspen found a letter in the back of the bookstore she owns. The letter was from a woman telling her lover to make sure to hide the loot well. After some digging, she discovered the letter was from Patricia Hall to her lover, Robert Adams. Robert Adams was actually the Black Hat Bandit. In 1955, he robbed the Hastings National Bank in Nebraska."

"How much did he steal?"

"Fifty-thousand dollars."

He whistles. "Fifty-thousand dollars? That'd be worth about half a million in today's money."

"Anyway, Aspen and Ashlyn decided they were going to locate the 'missing loot' as they referred to it. They followed the clues and ended up discovering the money hidden near an old railroad station."

"Correction," Juniper hollers from behind us. "I'm the one who dug the money up."

I glance back at her. "There is no correction needed. I didn't say you didn't dig the money up."

She steps forward and hugs Beckett. "Welcome to the family."

My lips purse. "It's a bit premature to welcome him to the family."

Maverick kisses my cheek. "Hi, Lilac."

I'm stunned by him kissing me and flustered about what I should say. "Hi?" The word comes out sounding like a question.

Beckett wraps an arm around me and pulls me near. "Hey, Maverick."

"Are you ready for this?" Maverick asks.

"Of course, we're ready," I answer. "I was here yesterday before the pub quiz helping Aspen set everything up."

Maverick stares at me in confusion for a moment and I wonder what I've done wrong this time, but, after a moment, he winks at me. "Sounds good."

We continue our journey toward *Fall Into A Good Book,* Aspen's bookstore. When we turn onto Main Street, I note there's a crowd waiting outside the bookstore.

"Aspen and Ashlyn will be pleased."

When no one responds to my comment, I glance behind me to discover Juniper and Maverick gone. "Where did they go?"

"Psst." Juniper waves at me from the entrance to the back alley. "We're going in the rear entrance of the bookstore."

"Okay," I say as I follow her.

Maverick pulls out a ballcap and sunglasses. "What do you think?" he asks and wiggles his eyebrows.

"I think you appear disheveled," I tell him since the fake hair attached to the ballcap is a mess. "And the sunglasses are overkill. I'm also confused as to why you're attempting to hide your identity. Everyone in Winter Falls knows who you are."

"The paps," Juniper says.

"The paps? What are the paps?"

"The paparazzi. Didn't you notice the news vans?"

I'm confused. Why is the location of a movie star news? "You don't mean the actual evening news would be interested in Maverick Langston's location?"

"We can't chance it," Maverick says before leading Juniper to the rear entrance of the bookstore.

I retrieve my key for the door, but it bangs open before I can locate it.

"Thank Litha, you're here." Aspen motions us inside. "I need help."

"What do you need us to do?" Juniper asks.

"Not you. Sorry, Juniper, but you need to be able to escape at a moment's notice if anyone recognizes Maverick."

She frowns, but Maverick leans over and kisses her hair. "I can leave now if you want."

She grabs his hand. "No. You're family. This is a family event. I want you here."

"Can you help man the cash register?" Aspen asks me.

"I assume this is a rhetorical question since I updated your point of sale operations."

"And you can greet people at the door," she tells Beckett who nods in response.

She claps her hands. "Let's do this!" She charges toward the door separating the back storage room from the store. I don't follow her. Instead, I clasp Beckett's hand and hold him back until we're alone.

He cocks an eyebrow at me. "What's wrong?"

"You don't have to help."

"I'm happy to." He winks and hauls me to the store before I have a chance to respond.

He leads me to the cash register. "Stay here. If you get overwhelmed, send me a sign."

"A sign? What kind of sign?"

"Send me a text message and I'll come save you."

I bristle. "I'm not a damsel in distress. I don't need saving."

He tweaks my nose. "Of course not. It's still my privilege to rescue you."

"Everyone in their spots. We're about to open!" Aspen shouts.

Beckett kisses my forehead before sauntering to the front door to welcome visitors. Aspen thrusts a tray with glasses of champagne into his hands before unlocking the door.

For the next hour, he smiles and charms every person who walks in the door.

"I like him," Mom announces from next to me.

"You always like our boyfriends."

"Boyfriend? You admit you're involved?"

I shrug. I can hardly deny it when he showed up here today wearing the same clothes he had on yesterday. A piece of information the gossip gals enjoyed announcing to the entire store when they arrived forty-five minutes ago. Plus, we arrived together.

Sage slams her hand down on the counter. "Of course, they're involved. The question is when Beckett is going to pop the question."

"Pop the question? What question?"

She rolls her eyes. "*The* question."

"She means propose," Feather explains.

My brow furrows. "Propose? But we've been dating for less than twenty-four hours."

Cayenne snorts. "You go ahead and tell yourself it's only been twenty-four hours."

"Because it has been. We agreed to be in a relationship last night, which is less than twenty-four hours ago."

"Yes!" Petal shouts. "I win!"

Several people in the crowd look over at her shout. Before I know what's happening, half of the town is jammed around the counter.

"Sorry, ladies," Beckett says as he grasps my elbow. "I need to borrow her for a minute."

"You go ahead, Becky boy," Sage says.

Beckett leads me to the storage room and shuts the door behind us.

"You okay?"

"Why wouldn't I be?"

"Because those ladies were asking you questions you find uncomfortable."

"You don't think it's weird I find their questions uncomfortable?"

"Why is it weird? There's no right or wrong way to being comfortable."

He's obviously not spent enough time with my family. "What if I'm uncomfortable in situations everyone else thinks are normal?"

He shrugs. "What's normal?"

"Everyone else."

He growls before grasping my jaw and tilting my head until I'm forced to look him in the eye. "I don't know who told you

you're not normal, but don't you listen to them. Normal is in the eye of the beholder."

"I thought beauty was in the eye of the beholder."

He smiles and his eyes crinkle. This close I can see the flecks of gray in his blue eyes. "I'm trying to tell you I don't give a shit if you're normal. I love you, Lilac Bean, just the way you are."

His lips press against mine in a barely there kiss. "Now, you sorted?"

I nod. I think I am. No one's ever told me they like me just the way I am, let alone love me. Besides my family, of course. But they have to love me.

Can I trust Beckett to truly love me? I know he said he loves me last night, but I don't know if I believed him then. But he loves me for who I am? I might be convinced he was being truthful after all.

"We better get out there before one of those old biddies listening at the door has a heart attack."

"Who you calling old biddy?" Sage shouts through the door.

Beckett winks and mouths *told you so.*

Chapter 25

Ambiguous – when two parties make an agreement, but one person is deliberately vague about their acquiescence so as to create multiple interpretations of said agreement

BECKETT

Lilac crosses her arms over her chest and refuses to move. "I am not driving to work with you."

"Why not? We're both going to the same place. And it will save on energy consumption."

"You cannot seduce me with energy savings. We agreed to keep our relationship secret in the office."

An agreement I'm now regretting. I rub a hand down my face. No, I'm not regretting it. I don't want Lilac's career to be in jeopardy. What she doesn't realize is I won't let her career be affected.

"Now go." She shoos me out of her apartment.

"Promise me, you'll be right behind me and drive safe."

"I will promise no such thing. One, you need to return to your apartment for appropriate work attire."

I glance down at my jeans and t-shirt. Damn. I nearly forgot. I blame Lilac. She rolled out of bed this morning and tossed the t-shirt she slept in, in my direction, before raising an eyebrow at me over her shoulder. How could I resist chasing her into the bathroom? I couldn't. But now I'm late and not dressed for work.

"And two, I don't need anyone to tell me to drive safe. I am a safe driver."

"You don't get it, Lilac. I don't tell you to drive safe as an order. I tell you to drive safe because I worry about you."

Her nose wrinkles and she looks adorably confused. "Oh."

I soothe a finger over the smattering of freckles on her checks. "Yeah. Oh."

She clears her throat. "And, three, we agreed to keep our relationship secret at the office. Arriving on Monday morning in the same car is suspicious."

I drop my hand. She's got me there. I kiss her forehead. "Okay, Lilac, you win this round."

"This round? Our relationship is not a boxing match."

I wiggle my eyebrows. "I wouldn't mind sparring with you."

"You want to hit me in the face? This is most disturbing."

"I meant the rolling around naked kind of sparring."

"Oh." A blush creeps up her cheeks. "I enjoy that kind of sparring as well."

I open her apartment door. "I'll see you at work."

When I arrive at the office an hour later, I stroll down the hallway intent on ensuring Lilac arrived safely before going to my office. My plans are waylaid when Brandi rushes up to me.

"Finally! I was getting worried about you."

I check my watch. Despite the detour to my house to change, I'm barely five minutes late.

She grasps my hand and tugs me toward my office. I shake off her hold. What has gotten into her this morning?

I shove my hands in my pants pockets to prevent her from touching me again. When I reach my office and start to shoulder the door shut, Brandi stops me by following me inside.

"You have a ton of messages," she says and tries to hand me a stack of notes.

I motion for her to set the stack on my desk before shrugging off my suit jacket and hanging it up on the coat rack in the corner. As I'm rolling up my sleeves, I note Brandi sitting in a chair across from my desk.

"What are you doing?"

"Waiting for your instructions." She widens her eyes and licks her lips.

Crap. I should have known better than to flirt with my personal assistant. I rub a hand down my face as I contemplate how to handle the situation. Honesty's the best policy as Lilac would say.

"I'm afraid you got the wrong impression." Because of me being a complete and total idiot.

Her eyelashes flutter. "Wrong impression about what?"

"About our relationship."

She bends forward and juts out her chest, revealing her cleavage. "Yes?"

"There is no relationship between us except employer and employee."

Her bottom lip curls. "But I thought…"

"As I said, I'm afraid I gave you the wrong impression."

The whiney girl disappears, and her eyes sharpen as they narrow on me. "I'm contacting HR and lodging a sexual harassment complaint."

"That is your right. In the meantime, I'll arrange for you and Stan's PA to switch positions."

"What?" she screeches. "You can't demote me!"

"I'm not demoting you. Stan is a member of the board the same as I am, and his PA earns the same salary as you."

"But Stan's… He's …."

I wait. "Yes?" I ask despite knowing exactly what her problem is. Stan is happily married to a man and, therefore, not susceptible to Brandi's flirting attempts.

Knock! Knock!

"I don't mean to disturb," Lilac calls from her place at the doorway, "but we have a meeting scheduled to discuss the contract with Arkville."

Brandi rolls her eyes. "Of course, you do. All you do is talk about work."

Lilac is adorably confused. "Because we're in an office."

"Whatever. I'll be at HR." Brandi stomps off.

Lilac waits until she's gone before asking, "What's going on? Why is she meeting with HR?"

"Because I'm an idiot."

"You'll have to be more specific."

I grin. Lilac never fails to amuse me, even when she's being totally serious as she is now.

"Close the door."

She frowns. "I don't think closing the door is a good idea."

"Close and lock the damn door, Lilac."

She huffs but closes and locks the door.

I point to a chair. "Sit down."

"I thought you were going to be more accommodating now we're …" she pauses to ensure the door is closed, "in a personal relationship."

"Brandi is lodging a sexual harassment claim against me."

Her eyes widen. "What?" she barks before clearing her throat. "I meant what is the basis for her complaint? You flirting with her?"

I nod.

Her nose wrinkles. "Sexual harassment is the making of unwelcome and inappropriate sexual remarks or physical advances in the workplace."

"Flirting is inappropriate."

She stands. "This misunderstanding is all my fault. Let me speak with HR and straighten this out."

I catch her by the arm before she can go anywhere. I'm not letting her fall on her sword to save me. I'll deal with whatever consequences come my way. "No."

She glares at me. "You can't tell me what to do."

I don't remind her we're at work and I'm the boss here as my reminder will not go down well. "You rushing to my defense won't help matters."

She contemplates my words for a few moments. "Okay. But what happens now? Are you going to get fired?"

"I'm not going to get fired. Brandi will work with Stan from now on."

"Stan? The COO Stan?"

I nod.

"Are you quite certain you don't want me to speak to HR and sort this mess out? I can tell them I saw Brandi flirting with you and therefore your supposed advances were not unwelcomed."

I grasp her hand and lead her to the sofa in the corner of my office. She fights against my hold. "What are you doing?"

"I'm going to make out with the woman who's trying to save me."

"I told you there will be no kissing at the office."

"I agreed to no sex at the office. I didn't agree to no kissing."

Her jaw clenches and a fire sparks in her eyes. "We will be making all of our agreements in writing from now on. There is obviously too much ambiguity otherwise."

I tuck a strand of hair that escaped from her bun behind her ear. "I like ambiguity."

"I do not. Ambiguity leads to misunderstandings. Misunderstandings lead to injured parties."

I sit on the sofa and settle her in my lap. She crosses her arms over her chest and leans away from me.

"This is a bad idea. What if someone walks in?"

"No one walks into my office when the door's closed."

"I've walked in when the door was closed."

I cup her chin. "Except you. But you're already inside my office."

I nip her bottom lip and then soothe the bite with my tongue. She sighs and leans closer.

"I maintain this is a bad idea."

"The door's locked," I remind her.

I dip my head and drag my tongue along her neck. She tilts her chin back to offer me better access and I know I've got her where I want her now.

"If anyone catches us, I will seek retribution," she says.

I wiggle my eyebrows. "Oh yeah?"

"Have you met my sister Ashlyn?"

I shiver. Ashlyn reminds me of Cassandra who was a troublemaker from the moment she learned how to climb down the trellises outside her window.

"We won't get caught," I mumble against her lips and then I'm done talking because Lilac's right. We shouldn't be kissing in my office, but how can I resist her when she offered to defend me from HR? An action that would put her own position in jeopardy.

My tongue plunders her mouth and with her taste on my tongue, I forget all about work and careers and sexual harassment claims. Who cares about those mundane things when I have the woman I love pliant in my arms?

Chapter 26

Karaoke – can be alternately terrifying or a means to seduce your fiancé

"I'M GETTING MARRIED!" ASPEN shouts as I enter *Electric Vibes*.

Before I have a chance to remind her how her upcoming wedding nuptials are the reason for our gathering at the bar tonight, she tackles me to the floor. I push her off of me and stand.

"What is it with you and tackling me lately?" I ask as I brush debris off of my skirt.

"She better not tackle me," Ashlyn says as she enters behind me. She then turns to the side and poses with her arms in the air.

"What is she doing?"

"I'm showing off my baby bump. And look at these." She grabs her breasts and shoves them together. "They're growing. They're finally growing!"

Her best friend, Moon, bumps her hip. "It took them long enough."

They giggle and throw their arms around each other before rushing off.

"Have fun while you can," Ellery hollers after them. "The fun won't last when your baby's up all night screaming and crying."

Aspen frowns when she notices the bundle Ellery's carrying. "You brought your daughter to my bachelorette party?"

Ellery rolls her eyes. "What did you expect? You ordered Lyric to have his bachelor party on the same night as your bachelorette party. Where was Willow supposed to go?"

"With me." Mom sweeps in and steals the baby away. Ellery doesn't bother to protest.

"Why are we having this bachelorette party now?" I ask Aspen once Mom disappears into the crowd. "You're not getting married for several months."

"Does there need to be an excuse for a party?"

"My guess is she wants to start trying to get pregnant," Ellery says.

My brow furrows in confusion. According to my observations, Aspen has already been trying to get pregnant.

"New betting round," Sage yells from behind me and I startle. I should have been paying better attention to my surroundings. Letting your guard down in Winter Falls is never a good idea.

"What's this one for?" Feather asks.

"When will Aspen get pregnant," Sage says.

Petal looks Aspen up and down. "I can't believe she's not pregnant already. Lyric is a strapping young man."

I ignore them and address Ellery, "What is the protocol for the evening?"

"Protocol?"

"Yes, the protocol. We've decorated the bar, Aspen's wearing a sash declaring her the bride to be, what happens next?"

She threads her arm through mine. "Now, we get our drink on."

"You can't drink. You're breastfeeding."

"Let me introduce to you this wonderful invention called pumping." Before I have a chance to remind her I'm an engineer and am aware of what pumping is, Lennon slams a pitcher of margaritas down on the counter.

"I don't want any trouble from you West girls tonight," he waits until we nod before continuing, "unless it's fun, then make all the trouble you want."

"This is for the one who's preggers," he adds as he sets a pitcher of orange juice on the counter.

"Thanks, Lennon." Aspen launches herself over the bar and kisses him on the cheek.

"I like you, Aspen Cloud West. Even if you are marrying the po-po."

She shrugs. "I loved Lyric before he became the po-po."

"Po-po schmo-po. Lyric won't arrest any of us." Ashlyn dismisses the idea with a wave of her hand.

"Are you making up words again?" I ask her.

"It's not made-up if it rhymes."

"And I *will* arrest any West girl who steals the vehicular beacon from the police and then parades up and down Main Street wearing it for a hat while singing *I shot the sheriff*," Lyric declares as he joins us.

Ashlyn bats her eyelashes. "I have no idea what you're referring to, Chief."

He crosses his arms over his chest. "It's on YouTube."

"Really? How many hits did I get?" She clears her throat. "I meant how many hits did *it* get?"

"What are you doing here?" Aspen asks before Lyric can answer Ashlyn. Her eyes widen when she notices the men gathered behind him. "What are all of you doing here?"

"You demanded I have my bachelor party the same night as your bachelorette's party. Where did you think we'd go?"

She shrugs. "I don't know. You could play poker at the house or have Mr. Moneybags fly you to New York City."

"Which one is Mr. Moneybags?" Cole asks.

She waves her hand vaguely toward Rowan, Maverick, and Beckett. "Any one of them will do."

I assume she's referring to Maverick or Rowan but when Beckett doesn't contradict her assumption, I study him. While it's true he's a CEO of a company, *Clean Mountain Environment* isn't especially big or prominent. I'm certain he makes a good wage, but moneybags implies a vast amount of wealth.

"Are you wealthy?" I ask him.

He coughs. "Um, what?"

"Are you wealthy?" I repeat, although he obviously heard my question the first time.

"Would it bother you if I were?"

"No, but why does Aspen know, and I don't?" I respond and wonder why he evaded my question.

Aspen snorts. "Have you seen his car? It retails at 200,000 dollars."

Cole ribs Maverick. "How much does your car cost?"

"Stop!" Ashlyn pushes her way into the middle of the group. "We can't decide who's the richest based on cars."

"Why not?" Juniper asks as she joins the party. "Because Rowan doesn't own a car?"

"Yes, exactly."

"I vote we stop talking about money since it's vulgar," Ellery suggests, and I nod.

"Good idea. I believe we're here to celebrate with the future bride." My brow wrinkles. "And the future groom? I'm uncertain what's happening here."

Beckett tags my hand and pulls me near before kissing my forehead. "Hello, honey," he whispers against my hair, and I melt into him.

I smile up at him. "Hi."

My gaze is torn from his when Aspen shouts, "Karaoke contest."

"Boys against girls," Juniper adds.

My heart begins to race and catching my breath becomes difficult. I grasp Beckett's hands when I feel dizziness hit. I do not enjoy singing on a stage in front of other people. Public speaking is not an issue for me but singing? Singing is not one of my talents. And performing acts I'm not proficient at in public makes me anxious.

Aspen wrenches me away from Beckett and drags me through the bar with my other sisters trailing after us until we reach the bathroom. "Are you okay?"

"I don't want to sing on stage."

"It's okay. You don't have to."

"But it's a contest." Any contest in the family means I have to participate. Those are the rules.

"I'll go twice," Juniper volunteers.

"We might have a chance at winning this thing if Lilac doesn't sing," Ellery says. "Sorry, Lilac."

"No need to apologize. I understand my talents do not lie in singing." Thus, the entire reason I'm panicking.

"I veto. I want Lilac to sing. Come on, Lilac," Ashlyn pleads with me. "You need to go up there and sing to Beckett."

Her reasoning is flawed. "Why? Beckett loves me for who I am."

"What?" she screeches before flinging herself into my arms. "I'm so happy for you."

I pat her back. "Thank you?"

Aspen drags me away from my baby sister. "It's agreed. Lilac won't sing." She rubs her hands together. "Now, we need to get back out there. We have a karaoke contest to win."

Beckett is waiting in the hallway outside of the restroom when we exit. He steps forward when he sees me. "Are you okay?"

"Everything is fine."

"With any other woman, I'd be terrified if she told me everything's fine."

"Why? What's wrong with the word fine?"

He smiles. "Absolutely nothing." He wraps an arm around me, and we follow my sisters back to the main area of the bar.

"Me first," Aspen shouts and jumps on the stage before stealing the microphone from Lennon. "You know the song."

We push a few tables together in front of the stage and settle in to listen to Aspen sing *Light My Fire.*

"Why does Lyric appear ready to jump on the stage and haul Aspen away?" Beckett asks.

"It's the song they lost their virginity to," I explain. Rowan, Cole, and Maverick scowl at me while Beckett laughs. "What's wrong? Sex is perfectly natural."

He settles his arm around my shoulders and plays with my hair. "Men prefer not to think of the woman they consider their sister losing her virginity."

"Oh, I apologize."

The song finishes and Lyric springs onto the stage. He rips the microphone from Aspen's hand and drops it on the ground before throwing her over his shoulder and storming off.

"Welp. That's one way to do a mic drop," Ashlyn says when all the hooting and hollering calms down.

I look around at the table. We're now short two people. "How are we going to have a contest when two of the contestants have left?"

Maverick stands. "It doesn't matter. I'm winning this thing right now."

"What are you doing?" Juniper hisses after him. "Someone will recognize you."

He winks. "Tonight is for locals only."

"Don't worry, Rickie," Sage hollers from her position by the door. "We got you covered."

I scan the room and realize I know every single person in the bar tonight. Maverick's correct. There are no tourists here tonight.

Juniper bites her bottom lip. "Are you sure?"

He picks up a guitar and settles on a stool. "This is for my June Bug."

He strums the strings and begins to sing the song he wrote for my sister, *Stay For Forever.*

By the time he finishes, Juniper's dashing a finger under her eyes. *Thank you* she mouths to him. He winks before clearing his throat.

"Ahem. As many of you know, this song convinced Juniper to finally take a chance on me and move in with me." He pauses while people shout out their agreement. "So, I figured maybe it'd be the song to convince her to marry me."

Juniper gasps before slapping her palms to her cheeks.

"June Bug, will you stay with me for forever as my wife?"

My fingers dig into Beckett's leg as I wait for her to answer. While Juniper fooled everyone else, I observed her misery for months when she thought Maverick had cheated on her. She had a hard time letting him into her heart after his betrayal. I hold my breath as I wait for her to answer. I can't watch her be depressed for months again.

"Yes," she whispers and then stands before shouting, "Yes! Maverick Langston, I'll marry you!"

She springs onto the stage while he jumps off and they collide before falling to the floor. They're laughing, so I assume they're uninjured.

"Your family's awesome, Lilac," Beckett says as he grasps my chin and tilts my head up. When he notices the tears leaking from my eyes, he wipes them away with a smile on his face. He kisses my eyelids and I squeeze his wrists.

"But not as awesome as you are, Lilac."

I'm done waiting and lift up to touch his lips to mine. I can feel his smile against my lips, and I smile in return.

"What did we miss?" Lyric's yell interrupts our kiss.

Beckett pulls his lips from mine and bursts into laughter.

At his laughter, some of the fear of him tiring of dealing with my issues dissolves. Maybe this is the man who will stay. Only one time is in the past.

Chapter 27

Proof – when the man you love acts in such a way as to establish he's the man for you

"Are you ready for our date?" Beckett asks when I open my door to him.

I look down at my outfit. I'm wearing jeans and a white button-up shirt. "I believe I'm ready. You didn't mention what we're doing so I was unsure as to what to wear."

He kisses my cheek. "You look gorgeous."

Gorgeous? I admit I'm not altogether bad looking but gorgeous?

He chuckles. "Accept the compliment."

"Thank you."

He shakes his head at me before motioning toward my purse. "Grab your stuff and let's go."

I grab my purse and laptop bag, but he snatches the laptop bag from me. "No. This is a date, not a work engagement. You don't need your laptop. In fact, you don't need your phone."

"Don't need my phone? Is this some kind of joke? How can I reference past events or research any questions that may arise? What if I need a phone number? What if there's an emergency?" I feel panic bubbling up inside of me.

He soothes a hand over my shoulder and the panic immediately recedes at his touch. "Forget I said anything. You can bring your phone with you."

"Of course, I can. I don't need your permission."

He smiles as he leads me out of the building to his car.

Once we're driving out of town, I ask, "Where are we going?"

"It's a surprise."

"I'm not a fan of surprises."

"Because you prefer to be prepared for all eventualities."

I narrow my eyes on him. "How do you know?"

He grasps my hand and places our clasped hands on my thigh. "You're pretty easy to figure out."

"I am?" People usually say the opposite. I'm confusing. I don't follow social norms. I do what's least expected.

"Well, honey, you're easy for me to figure out."

This is most unexpected. I'll have to think on it later. Meanwhile, I have a list of questions to ask him during our date to ensure conversation flows. According to my research, silence should be avoided during a date.

"Why did you relocate to White Bridge?"

"For the job. *Clean Mountain Environment* recruited me."

"And you moved to Colorado from Saint Louis?"

"Me and my sisters. Well, three of my sisters."

"You've mentioned raising four sisters several times, but you don't talk about your fourth sister. Is there a reason why not? And why didn't she move with you?"

"Olivia is the oldest of the girls. She's three years younger than me. When Mom and Dad died, she thought she was old enough to go off on her own."

"She would have been fifteen. Fifteen is still a child."

"Try telling Olivia that. She was stubborn as all get out and hellbent on being independent. I can't count the number of times the police brought her home after catching her shoplifting or drunk."

I squeeze his hand. "I'm sorry. It couldn't have been easy for you. Between raising your sisters and dealing with Olivia, when did you have time to grieve the loss of your parents?"

"I didn't. After Gabrielle graduated from high school and went off to college, I went through a bad patch."

"What's a bad patch?"

"Drinking, gambling, raising hell. Getting into trouble any way I could."

I'm uncertain what he means by getting into trouble, but the details aren't important.

"And now?"

"I went to counseling, got my shit together."

"But your sisters worry about you, so they followed you to Colorado?" I surmise.

He nods. "Exactly."

"What about Olivia? She didn't come with you."

"She wasn't leaving Saint Louis for some Podunk town."

"Podunk town? White Bridge isn't a small town. It has a population of over one-hundred thousand."

"To her, it's provincial."

"She would hate Winter Falls."

He shrugs. "We'll see. You'll meet her at Christmas."

Christmas is months away. And he's assuming we'll still be together then. I smile. All signals are indicating taking a chance on Beckett was worth the risk.

"Now, for your first surprise." He indicates a wind turbine. "Ta da!"

"It's a wind turbine." I study it for a minute. "It's a General Electric 1.5 megawatt model. Its blades are 116 feet long and the tower is 212 feet tall. It weighs in at over 164 tons. The tower alone weighs about seventy-one tons."

Beckett brings the car to a stop near the tower. "And we're going inside it."

"We are? I've always wanted to tour the inside of one."

I missed my chance in college as Ashlyn was performing in the high school play on the day my class was scheduled to tour one. She was the lead in the play, and I couldn't miss it. Had I known my baby sister would go on to study drama in college and perform in hundreds of plays, I would have skipped the high school play.

While I've been gazing at the wind turbine, Beckett exited the car and is now holding my door open for me. He offers me his hand and helps me out. He brings me flush to him and kisses me quickly before leading me toward the rear of the car.

He opens the trunk and hands me a helmet with a light and a climbing harness.

"We're going all the way to the top?" The harness is unnecessary otherwise.

I don't wait for him to answer before stepping into my climbing harness and affixing the helmet atop my head.

"What's wrong?" he asks when he notices me bouncing from foot to foot. "Got ants in your pants?"

"Of course not. Where would I find ants? And why would they be in my pants? I'm excited."

He chuckles as he motions me toward the wind turbine where a man is awaiting our arrival.

For the next hour, we take a tour of the turbine. There's some climbing included and it's hot and humid inside, but I don't care. I ask our tour guide question after question, but he doesn't seem to mind my inquisitiveness. In fact, when we shake hands at the end of the tour, he offers me a job.

"We can always use people like you at our company," he says.

Beckett wraps an arm around my waist and pulls me near. "She's not looking for a new position."

The man lifts his hands in surrender as he steps back.

We take our leave and remove our equipment to place it in the trunk. I remove my shirt, too as I'm hot and sweaty and the outside temperature has increased.

"If I had known you were wearing a cute little tank top underneath your shirt, I would have switched on the heat on our way here," Beckett says before pulling me into his arms and placing a hard kiss on my lips.

I mewl in protest when he pulls away.

He winks. "On to our next surprise."

"You mean the picnic lunch?"

"How did you know?"

"There's a picnic basket in the backseat of your car. Since it wasn't there the last time I was in your car, I assume you placed it there today. Also, I can smell fried chicken."

He chuckles. "I should have known better than to think you wouldn't notice the basket."

"Yes, you should have. I'm quite observant."

We settle in the car, and he begins driving again. "Where are we having this picnic?"

"I thought near the waterfall in Winter Falls. I've heard it's quite lovely there."

"It is lovely, but who have you heard this from? Did Ashlyn set this up? Because if she did, I can guarantee she'll crash our picnic. The whole family will."

He frowns.

"Ashlyn suggested we go on a picnic today, didn't she?"

"I should have known better," he grumbles. "Cassandra and her could be twins."

I don't disagree. "Where shall we go instead?"

"There's a park near my house," he suggests.

"And what are the chances of your sisters discovering us there?"

"High." He runs a hand down his face. "I should have never told them how I feel about you."

"You told them you love them? Why?"

He checks his rearview mirrors before pulling to the side of the road and turning to face me. "Why wouldn't I tell them? Are you embarrassed of me?"

"Me? Embarrassed of you? You can't be serious."

"Why else would you not want me to tell my sisters how I feel?"

"I didn't say I didn't want you to tell them. I asked why you told them."

He sighs. "With any other woman, I'd say semantics, but you're perfectly serious."

"I don't understand this saying semantics business. Do you say semantics and then the discussion is over? How does saying one word end a discussion?"

"Never mind," he mutters before cradling my face in his hands. "To answer your question, I'm close with my sisters and they bugged me until I admitted my feelings." I feel the corners of my lips turn up at his admission. "Now, have you told your sisters you love me yet?"

"No. I don't share my feelings easily. This annoys my family."

"Are you ready to share your feelings with me?"

Does he want me to confess I love him? He did ask if I had told my sisters I love him. Obviously, he is under the impression I love him. He is correct, although I don't know how he knows. I haven't told him. I don't plan to keep my feelings secret forever, but I have not yet decided when or how I want to reveal this knowledge to him.

"It's fine, Lilac. You can take your time."

"I can? Most people, including my family, are annoyed with how reticent I am to discuss emotions."

He kisses my nose, "Lilac, I love all of you and I know you. I know how difficult feelings are for you. Don't worry. You're not getting rid of me that easily."

His words are yet another indicator of the good choice I've made in letting him into my life. I open my mouth to tell him I love him, but the words still won't come.

He smiles and lets me go to switch on the engine, "Shall we go have our picnic now?"

Yes, Beckett Dempsey is the man for me. Grumpy boss and all.

Chapter 28

Coincidences – do not exist according to Lilac

BECKETT

I stop on Lilac's parents' porch and turn to address my sisters. "I want all of you on your best behavior today."

Cassandra rolls her eyes at me, but before she has a chance to answer, the door flies open.

"Why do they have to behave?" Ashlyn asks. "We're a strict no behaving household."

I nod to her belly. "I can't wait until you have a teenager, and we remind him or her of those words."

"No worries." She beams at me. "Rowan's going to be the hard ass. I'm going to be the cool mom."

"And if you have a girl?"

"What difference does the gender of our child make?"

I chuckle. "You'll see."

Lilac arrives and her brow wrinkles in that adorable way she has. "Why is everyone standing on the porch? Did Juniper bring her dog and it has flatulence?"

"My dog does not have flatulence," Juniper shouts from inside the house.

"Ha! You are such a liar!" Ashlyn rushes off to confront her sister.

"Why has no one properly welcomed you?" Lilac asks.

"He's family. He doesn't need to be welcomed into the house," her mom, Ruby, says.

"Family means—"

"These must be your sisters," her mom says, cutting off the lecture Lilac was no doubt about to give on the proper definition of family.

Ruby ushers my sisters into the house and shuts the door behind her leaving us standing alone on the porch. Lilac marches toward the door, but I capture her hand and draw her to me.

"Hi, honey," I whisper against her lips. She sighs and I thrust my tongue past her lips. I drop her hand to wrap my arms around her as I explore her mouth. Her fingers dig into my shoulders, and I shove my hard length into her belly.

She moans and I hitch her leg over my hip. The door opens behind me.

"Here, in case you need some."

I rip my mouth from Lilac's to discover Ruby laying a package of condoms on the porch. I groan and place my forehead against Lilac's.

"No fair, Mom," Ashlyn shouts. "You know I had twenty bucks on him getting her shirt off before she remembered she was on the porch."

Ruby winks at us before shutting the door and returning inside.

I lower Lilac's leg to the floor and kiss her nose. "You ready to go inside?"

She clears her throat. "I am, but are you?" Her gaze dips to the erection pushing against the front of my shorts. "Do you need me to recite non-sexy things until it goes down?"

I chuckle. "What non-sexy things do you have in mind?"

She fishes her phone out of her pocket. "I have the quarterly results here. We can go over the figures."

Thinking about this week's board meeting to discuss the results of the second quarter and the projections for the third quarter is exactly what I needed. "I'm good."

I open the door and motion inside. "Shall we?"

"Where are Gabrielle and Elizabeth?" I ask as I look around at the room full of people. A room my two younger sisters are absent from.

"Gabrielle had a panic attack when Rowan stood up to introduce himself and she realized what a behemoth he is and ran into the kitchen. Elizabeth went with her," Ashlyn answers.

"Dream girl," Rowan growls.

"What? I'm merely telling him what happened."

Juniper snorts. "Liar. Gabrielle's fine," she tells me. "She's helping Mom in the kitchen."

"But she did say Rowan is a behemoth."

Juniper throws her arms in the air. "I give up!"

Ashlyn bows. "My work here is done."

"I'll go check on them."

Cassandra grunts. "You don't need to check on them. They're not children. They're fine."

Lilac squeezes my hand. "I'll go."

Ashlyn waits until Lilac enters the kitchen to speak. "Good. Ms. Fuddy Duddy is gone. Now, we can discuss the bets."

"What bets?" I don't know why I ask. Every bet I've learned of in Winter Falls thus far has been a gross violation of privacy.

"When will Juniper and Maverick get married?"

"Hello!" Ellery raises her hand. "Cole and I are getting married first."

Cole cocks an eyebrow. "We are? I thought you forgot about my proposal since you refuse to discuss a date."

"I didn't 'refuse' to discuss a date. I told you I can't set a date until Aspen does."

"Thanks, Ellery." Aspen blows her sister a kiss.

"Since Aspen has set a date, it's time for us to set our date."

"Any chance you can tell us the date now?" Ashlyn asks. "And we'll pretend to not know when you announce it."

"So, you can win all the bets about the date?" Ellery snorts. "No way."

"I'll share my winnings with you."

Ellery sighs. "Why are you dead set on winning? You don't need the money."

Ashlyn crosses her arms over her chest and sticks her bottom lip out. "Because Sage wins every single bet. The woman knows everything going on in town. I wouldn't be surprised if she keeps track of our ovulation schedules."

"You're pregnant. You're no longer ovulating," Lilac says as she returns to the living room.

I shake my head.

"What? Does talk of pregnancy and ovulation embarrass you?"

"Gee, Lilac. Way to induct the man into the family," Lyric grumbles as he enters the house.

Aspen checks her watch. "I didn't think you were going to make it in time to eat."

"I didn't think I would either."

"What happened?" Ashlyn asks with wide eyes. I don't know her well, but I know the look. It's the same one Olivia had each and every time the police brought her home.

Lyric frowns, apparently, he's familiar with the look as well. "Someone made a hole in the fence out at my brother's farm and all his goats got loose."

"Wasn't me," Juniper and Ashlyn shout at the same time.

Lyric ignores them. "Those goats got everywhere."

"They didn't get into the wildlife refuge, did they?" Juniper asks, but she's already walking toward the door. "I'll be back."

Maverick catches her before she reaches the door. "We'll be back."

Ashlyn sighs. "You know we're not going to see them again today."

"Lucky them," Ellery mutters.

"Anyway," Lyric clears his throat. "I've spent the past four hours rounding up Phoenix's goats."

"Phoenix is your brother?" Gabrielle asks.

"One of my younger brothers," Lyric explains. "Have you met him?"

"We did," Cassandra answers on Gabrielle's behalf. "As I recall, his goat took quite a liking to Gabrielle's skirt."

Gabrielle's cheeks darken and she ducks her head to hide her face behind her hair. Is she embarrassed or is she remembering Phoenix who she appeared interested in at the time?

She clears her throat and asks, "Did you find all the goats?"

"All but one. Of course, the one we couldn't find is Phoenix's favorite goat."

"He has a favorite goat?"

"It's the one he brings to all the Winter Falls' celebrations. It's probably the one that decided to eat your skirt for lunch."

"You mean Pan. Pan's missing? Oh no. We should go help."

"I'm sure Pan is fine. The little shit was probably hiding from Phoenix. Let me call him and ask." Lyric winks at Gabrielle before walking off while dialing his phone.

"Since when do you like goats?" Cassandra asks, and I have to remind myself tackling my sister is a bad idea.

"I like goats," Ashlyn says before skipping to Gabrielle. "Come on. Let's go talk about goats in the kitchen."

"You better not nibble on the fried chicken while you're in there," Ruby hollers after them.

Ashlyn winks at me before she disappears behind the door.

Ruby grunts. "She's going to eat the chicken."

Before she can follow them, the sliding door to the back porch opens and a man enters the house. "It's about time you returned, Daniel," Ruby says before she rushes to him. "Come meet Lilac's beau."

"Beau? This is not 18th Century France and Beckett is not my suitor come to meet my father to ask for his approval."

"Why not?" I ask Lilac.

"Suitor is someone who pursues a relationship with a view toward marriage."

I smirk. "I'm aware."

"You would want to marry me?" Her brow wrinkles and I reach forward to soothe it with my finger.

"Of course, I want to marry you. I love you."

What does she think I'm doing? Playing around with her? Lilac isn't a woman to play around with. She's a woman you take home to meet your family. I glance around the room and notice my sisters watching the interaction with interest. Maybe I need to buy Olivia a plane ticket to visit, so she can meet Lilac, too.

"But…"

I raise an eyebrow. "But?"

"But you're you." She waves a hand up and down in front of me. "And I'm me."

"And we fit perfectly together."

"I like him," her father declares. He holds out his hand. "I'm Daniel West."

"Beckett Dempsey."

His hand squeezes mine to the point of pain. "If you hurt my Lilac, I'll dig out my shotgun."

Lilac wrestles our hands apart. "You don't own a shotgun, Dad. You're a peace activist, remember?"

"A peace activist can get violent when it comes to protecting his family."

I wrap an arm around Lilac and draw her near. "Don't worry, Daniel. I won't hurt Lilac."

She melts into me, and I wink down at her. She smiles up at me and I realize I'll do anything to see her smile up at me this way for the rest of my life. I not only love the woman, she has my heart in her hands. I hope she's careful with it.

Chapter 29

Trick someone — only effective in the event you force a person to do something she doesn't want to do

My office door clicks closed, and I glance up to find Beckett standing in front of the door.

"What are you doing?" I ask despite knowing exactly what he's doing.

This is the third time he's come to my office today. I've managed to rebuff him each time, but I don't know how long I can resist him. I've always prided myself on being able to control my emotions but against Beckett, my control doesn't stand a chance.

He waggles his eyebrows. "What do you think?"

"I think we decided to keep our relationship a secret in the office, but everyone is going to figure it out if you keep coming into my office and shutting the door."

"It's nearly six. Everyone's distracted with getting ready to leave for the evening."

I check my watch. "It's barely five-thirty. There's another half an hour left of the workday."

Beckett saunters my way and rounds my desk before leaning against it next to me. He crosses his legs at his ankles and his arms over his chest. He looks completely relaxed. I, however, am not.

I shove at him. "What are you doing? You're too close to me."

"Honey, I can get much closer," he murmurs before sliding over until I'm forced to push my chair away from the desk.

He settles himself in front of me. "Much better."

"I don't know how this is better. I need to finish my work and now I can't reach my computer."

He braces his hands on my chair and leans forward until his face is mere inches from mine. "But now I can reach you and those luscious pink, pouty lips you have."

I stare at his lips as they come closer while his fingers drag up my arms leaving goosebumps in their wake. His lips have nearly met mine when my telephone rings.

I sigh in disappointment before reaching forward to answer it, but he snatches it away before I can.

"What are you doing?" I hiss. "I need to answer my phone."

"Promise me you'll come home with me tonight and I'll give you your phone."

"You could have asked me instead of holding my phone hostage."

He shrugs. "Would you have said yes?"

I'm confused by the question. Am I supposed to say no? Am I supposed to play hard to get? I don't play games.

"Of course, I would say yes. You're my boyfriend."

He kisses me on the nose and hands me my phone, which has stopped ringing in the meantime.

"I'll be ready to leave at six."

"I planned to work until seven."

"Six-thirty?"

I nod. I can compromise despite what my sisters think. Although, their idea of compromise is for me to do as they order. As usual, they don't understand the concept properly.

At 6:25 p.m., Beckett sashays back into my office. "Time to go."

I anticipated him arriving early and have nearly finished packing up. "I'll follow you."

He frowns. "Why? I'm not letting you go home tonight."

I raise an eyebrow. "Letting?"

"Don't worry. You'll be blinded with passion and won't mind a bit."

I don't bother contradicting his assertion since he's probably right. "I'll need a new set of clothes in the morning."

"Good thing you keep an extra set in your trunk in case of emergency, then, isn't it?"

I frown. "This isn't technically an emergency."

He glances behind him before stepping close and whispering to me, "When I tease you until you're begging me to come, you'll change your mind."

My breath catches in my throat. I've never enjoyed a lover teasing me before. Probably because I never allowed myself to truly let go the way I have with Beckett.

"I'll use the emergency clothes in my trunk," I pant.

He winks. "Thought you would."

He relieves me of my laptop bag before indicating the hallway. "After you, milady."

"I'm not an English noblewoman."

"But you're my queen," he claims as we exit the office.

After a brief debate, which he wins because saving energy is one of the purposes of my life, after all, we travel together in his car to his house. It's a ten-minute drive before we're pulling into the driveaway of a modern house. I notice the roof appears to be reflective.

"Are those solar panels?"

"Naturally. Although I also have a geothermal heating and cooling system, solar panels are essential for a net zero energy home."

Net zero energy home. I'm intrigued. I fling my door open. "What are you waiting for? I want the tour."

He chuckles as he meets me at the front of the car. "I'll give you the tour, but it's not very interesting. The house looks and feels the same as a normal home."

"Except it doesn't use any energy."

"It uses energy, but I produce more energy with the solar panels and geothermal HVAC than I use."

"Naturally. I would expect it to produce extra energy with both solar panels and a geothermal system," I say as I follow him toward the door.

"I use some of the excess to power my car and sell the rest to the local energy company," he says as he opens the door using a finger scanner.

"You have a biometric lock?"

"Yes, it's part of my home security. Don't worry. I can have my security guy come out and have your fingerprint added to the system."

I pause in the entryway. "What do you mean? Have my fingerprint added?"

"So you can enter the house. The code to enter doesn't work without fingerprint identification."

"I am aware of how biometric locking mechanisms work. What I don't understand is why you would add my fingerprint."

"I guess we're doing this now," he mumbles before leading me away from the doorway and into the living room.

The living room, kitchen, and dining area are an open concept with the entire back wall of the space covered in floor to ceiling windows. I ignore the furnishings and walk to the windows where I can see for miles since the view is unimpeded by other houses.

"How large is the property your house sits on?"

"Five acres. I bought the lots next door to me and the three lots behind mine."

I open my mouth to ask him how much the lots cost but shut it again when I remember Ellery telling me it's rude to ask people questions about money.

"Go ahead. Ask away."

"I believe my question may be conceived as rude."

"Ruder than asking me whether I'm having problems with defecation?"

I feel my cheeks warm at his question. "That question slipped out."

He chuckles. "What do you want to ask?"

"I was curious how much the lots cost, but it's none of my business."

"It is your business."

"No, I don't believe it is."

"Yes, it is." Before I have a chance to respond, he lifts his palm to stop me. "It's your business because everything about me is your business. This is how relationships work."

"This seems to be an advanced part of a relationship."

"Honey, I love you. We've reached the advanced part."

Is this the moment I tell him I love him? According to those romance books Aspen insists I read for our monthly book club, this appears to be a proper moment. We're alone. He said he loves me. I love him. All indicators are go. But I can't seem to get the words out, which is most unlike me.

Although most people believe omitting to tell the truth is not a lie, I do not ascribe to this view. I've always claimed not telling a person all of the facts is the same as a lie. Which means I should admit to Beckett that I love him. Otherwise, I'm lying. And I do not lie.

"In fact," while I've been debating with myself Beckett moved and is now standing in front of me, "I think we should move in together."

All thoughts of telling him my feelings are forgotten upon hearing this alarming statement. "What? Moving in together is a big step. In romance novels, the couple does not move in together until their relationship is certain."

He shrugs. "Okay."

I'm confused. "Okay? You're giving up?"

"Yep," he claims but there's a smirk on his face.

Why would he be smirking after giving up? I gasp when I realize why. "You think me changing my mind and agreeing to move in with you is a foregone conclusion."

He doesn't deny it. "Honey, I saw the way your eyes lit up when you saw the solar panels."

"I'm an environmental engineer. I'm interested in ways to make a home energy efficient."

"And when I mentioned geothermal HVAC, you practically drooled."

"I did not!" I clear my throat when I realize I nearly shrieked and lower my voice. "I'm not ready to move in with you."

"Why not?"

"Because it's too quick." And I'm not yet convinced he won't tire of me and my social ineptitude.

"Okay." Once again, he gives in easily.

"Is this a trick? You never give in easily. And, yet, you've done it twice now."

He shrugs. "Maybe I have better things to do." He removes the rubber band holding my hair in place and runs his hands through the strands.

"Such as?"

"Something I've been dying to do since the day I met you."

He gathers my hair in his fist and jerks my head back until my neck is exposed. He nibbles and bites his way along it until he reaches my jaw. I try to move so I can kiss him, but I'm immobilized by his hold on me. I'm surprised to find myself excited by the notion of being restrained.

"I've got you right where I want you," he whispers in my ear before swirling circles with his tongue around the skin behind my ear. My knees weaken and I grab hold of the lapels of his jacket before I fall. He smirks before nipping my bottom lip.

"Why are all—" Cassandra cuts herself off. "Oops. We'll come back later."

"Why are we coming back later?" Elizabeth asks. "You promised me dinner."

Beckett releases his hold on my hair and tucks me under his arm in time for me to see Elizabeth enter the dining room. Her eyes widen. "Oh."

"Why is everyone crowding the entryway?" Gabrielle asks as she pushes past her sisters. She waves at me. "Hi, Lilac. I didn't realize you were joining us for dinner."

"I didn't realize they were joining me for dinner," Beckett grumbles before kissing my hair and releasing me. "What does everyone want to eat?" he asks as he strides toward the kitchen.

When I don't immediately follow him, he urges me forward. "Come on, Lilac. You don't want to keep my sisters waiting for food."

Cassandra shoves him. "Don't make us sound bad."

"Too late. Lilac's family now. She'll figure out what pigs you are soon enough."

Family now? He says the words as if they're not significant. But they are significant. He's the first person outside of my biological family to accept me for who I am. I need to tell him I love him. He said he loved me just as I am before, and I'm beginning to realize he means it.

Chapter 30

Lie – only untrue until you change someone's mind

BECKETT

"Here you go."

I glance up to find Brandi entering my office and scowl at her.

"What are you doing here?"

We're not supposed to have any contact until HR finishes its investigation into her sexual harassment complaint. We both know the complaint is bullshit, but rules are rules as Lilac would say.

"Just making sure you're ready for today's board meeting," she says with a smirk.

She's never been worried about me being ready for a meeting before despite having been my PA. I should have listened to Lilac and fired the woman the first time she showed up for work fifteen minutes late wearing yesterday's clothes and smelling of a whisky distillery. I didn't and now I have to live with the consequences.

"Thank you," I begrudgingly thank the woman for the file she sets on my desk.

"See ya around." She waves as she leaves. "Or not."

I frown. She's acting stranger than usual. I let thoughts of Brandi go as I review the file to confirm I have all the information I need for the board meeting. I glance through the second quarter figures with a nod. It's all here.

I check the time. Fifteen minutes before the meeting begins. Just enough time to stop by Lilac's office and bother her.

She sighs when her office door clicks shut behind me. "You seriously don't understand the concept of keeping a secret."

"And you seriously don't understand the appeal of sneaking around."

She frowns at my words. "Am I appealing because I'm forbidden? Is that why you think you love me?"

I growl as I grasp her hands and haul her out of her chair. When her body is plastered to mine, I gaze into her eyes letting all of my love for her show.

"I love you because you're my Lilac who smells like honey, tastes like sin, and has passion inside of her reserved for my eyes only." Her eyes dilate at my words, but I'm not done. "I love you because you're smart, don't take anyone's shit, and are loyal to those you love."

"I—"

I place a finger over her lips to stop her from speaking. I know she loves me but is afraid to tell me. I'm okay with her hesitation. It will make the words that much sweeter when she finally speaks them.

"Kiss me and wish me good luck at my board meeting."

Her eyes narrow at my order, but she pushes up on her toes to brush a sweet kiss over my lips. "Good luck, but you do know luck doesn't exist."

"Sure, it does. I met you, didn't I?" I wink and walk out before she has a chance to respond. Luck is not a topic I'm willing to discuss with Lilac.

I enter the boardroom with a smile on my face. I nod to our chairman of the board, Leonard, before taking a seat next to Stan, the COO.

"How is Brandi working out?" I ask him.

He cringes. "How have you not fired her?"

I shrug as I'm unwilling to admit I'm a complete idiot who's been too busy falling in love over the past year to pay attention to my personal assistant.

Doris, the board secretary, and Norman, the CFO, enter the room and take their seats.

Leonard clears his throat. "Shall we begin? As we're all here."

Doris opens her notebook and nods at him to indicate she's ready.

"The first matter to discuss is the behavior of our CEO, Beckett Dempsey."

What? I quit rifling through my notes and whip my head up to look at Leonard. "Excuse me?"

"It has come to my attention that you've been accused of harassing an employee under your direct supervision."

I inhale a deep breath to calm myself before I lash out at the chairman of the board. Damnit. I knew not firing Brandi would come back to bite me in the ass.

"Human Resources is investigating the charge of sexual harassment. In the meantime, I've ensured the employee has no direct contact with me." In other words, I've followed the employee manual to the letter.

"The employee in question is currently working as my personal assistant and I've already reprimanded her twice," Stan adds. "You can review her employee record if you wish."

"It sounds as if the matter has been satisfactorily handled," Norman says. "Shall we move on to the Q2 numbers?"

I switch on the beamer to begin the presentation, but Leonard stops me. "Not so quick. I believe there is another matter to discuss."

When he doesn't indicate what the matter is, I ask, "Which is?"

"You having a relationship with an employee."

Crap. How did they find out about me and Lilac? Despite what she thinks, I've been discreet in the office. How should I respond? Do I deny the relationship? Do I ask who's been spreading rumors? Or do I admit I'm in love with one of our engineers?

Shit. I should have been prepared for this. But I was convinced no one knew about me and Lilac. She's going to lose it when she finds out. I need to make sure she never finds out.

"Perhaps you can explain." I need to know what he knows before I accidentally admit to things he's unaware of.

"You can deny it all you want, but I have a witness who has seen you and another engineer in the throes of passion in your office."

"The throes of passion?" Stan chuckles next to me.

I'm not finding anything amusing. Who saw us in my office? I always shut and lock the door when Lilac's with me. But there is one person who has a key besides me.

"Fuck. Brandi," I mutter.

Stan's eyes widen at the mention of my former PA. "Please tell me you're not screwing around with her. She'll stab you in the back the first chance she gets."

"She already has. She already has," I mutter under my breath before admitting to the room, "It's true. I'm in a relationship with Lilac West."

"I move we vote whether to remove Beckett Dempsey from his position as CEO of *Clean Mountain Environment*. Who seconds the motion?" Leonard looks around the room with a gleam in his eyes.

I knew he didn't approve of me from day one. It wasn't hard to figure out when he called me a city boy with no background in environmental engineering. I didn't realize his dislike would lead him to try to fire me, though. My mistake. Know your enemies is lesson one of management.

"Now, hold on." Stan holds up his hands. "Shouldn't we discuss the situation first?"

Leonard frowns. "What is there to discuss? Do you want details of what their encounters entail?"

Stan scoffs. "No, I don't want details of their sexual encounters. I want to know about their relationship."

Norman clears his throat. "I agree. We can reprimand him and move on to more important things if this was merely a one time thing such as having dinner together."

Fucking hell. Why did I ever brag about having dinner with Lilac in a meeting? Because I was a jealous idiot.

Leonard motions to me. "Go ahead."

I run a hand through my hair as I consider how I should answer. "Lilac West and I have been dating for approximately a month now."

"And Lilac is under your direct supervision?" Norman asks.

"Yes, she's an environmental engineer and is a project leader who reports directly to me."

"She should report to the Chief Technology Officer," Stan points out. "But that position has been open for over a year now."

"It's immaterial as to whether she should report to the CTO or not as there is no CTO and she's been reporting directly to Beckett who is carrying on a relationship with her," Leonard sums up.

"It's more than a relationship. We're in love and we plan to marry." At least, I plan to marry Lilac as soon as I can convince her to say yes.

He frowns. "That changes things. When is your wedding planned?"

Shit. I didn't think he'd ask me. "We haven't set a date yet." Technically I'm not lying. We haven't set a date yet.

"I've heard enough. I move we vote whether to remove Beckett Dempsey from his position as CEO of *Clean Mountain Environment*. Who seconds the motion?"

Norman raises his hand. "I second."

"Those in favor of removing Beckett Dempsey from his position raise your hands." He raises his hand and Norman joins him.

"Those opposed."

Stan and I raise our hands.

"You haven't voted," Leonard accuses Doris.

"I abstain."

Hell. We're in deadlock, which means the chairman of the board has the deciding vote.

"What about the shareholders?" I ask before Leonard can fire me.

"The shareholders have delegated the power to fire the CEO to this board."

I grind my teeth. "I am aware. Have you asked their opinion on this matter?"

"I'm confident they'll agree."

I wouldn't be so confident if I were him.

I throw out the only offer I have. "I'll agree to go on unpaid leave until you consult with the shareholders."

He frowns. "This is highly unusual. I have the power to remove you from your position."

"Yes," I agree. "But if the shareholders disagree with your decision, they have the power to reinstate me." Which I'm confident they will. "It will injure our image if I'm removed and then reinstated."

It will also weaken Leonard's authority. Ever since he was appointed Chairman of the Board last year, he's been obsessed with power. His obsession is about to come to an end, though. I'm going to make certain of it.

"It's a good compromise," Stan says.

Norman nods. "I agree."

Leonard grinds his teeth. "Fine," he grunts. "You'll take an unpaid leave of absence while I consult with the shareholders on the matter." When I don't move, he motions to the door. "Your leave of absence begins now."

I'm going to enjoy firing him, I think as I march out of the room.

Chapter 31

Heartbreak – something you have to experience to realize how painful it is

JACK POKES HIS HEAD in my office. "Did you hear?"

I frown at my colleague. Apparently, gossip hour has arrived. "No, I didn't." I don't listen to any of the rumors in the office. He should know this.

He rubs his hands together in excitement. "Beckett got the sack."

I feel my heart rate quicken as my lungs constrict making breathing difficult. "What?" I gasp out. "Beckett was fired? For what reason?"

"Rumor has it he was caught carrying on with an employee."

My lungs seize and breathing is no longer difficult. It's impossible. This is all my fault. This whole time I've been worried about my own career. I didn't consider how our relationship might affect Beckett's career. I believe my sisters would call me a selfish cow at this juncture.

I jump to my feet and my chair flies out behind me until it hits the wall with a thump. "Is he here? Has he left yet?"

"He's already gone. Don't you want to know who he's been having an affair with?"

My brow furrows in confusion. Doesn't everyone already know it's me? We had to have been found out. How else did Beckett get fired for breaching the fraternization policy?

Jack scans the hallway before stepping into my office and whispering, "I think it's Brandi."

"Brandi? Why do you think it's Brandi?"

He shrugs. "Who else could it be? You?" He chuckles but I fail to understand what's amusing. "Besides, she's been hitting on him since the day he arrived."

My shoulders sag in relief. No one knows I'm the one he's been having an affair with. In fact, if Jack is to be believed, no one suspects me at all. I shake my head. Once again, I'm only thinking of myself. I'll have to ask my sisters what's worse than a selfish cow.

"When did this happen?" How did this happen is the question I want to ask but don't dare.

"This morning. Beckett left straight after the board meeting."

Ah. Now I know why he hasn't bothered me all day. I've been missing him, but I didn't pick up the phone to check on him. It's becoming blatantly apparent how inept I am at being a partner in a relationship.

I begin packing up my things.

"What are you doing?"

I check the clock. It's only four o'clock. "I'm leaving for the day. I have a headache."

It's not a lie. The second Jack said Beckett was fired, my head began to ache. Jack replies, but I'm too busy trying to figure out how to handle the situation to listen to what he has to say. I wave at him as I rush down the hallway and out of the building.

I hurry to my car and drive to Beckett's house. I knock on the door, but he doesn't answer. I know he's here. His car is in the driveway, and I can see the lights on. He doesn't leave the lights on when he isn't in. It's impossible to have a zero energy house if you waste energy on lights you don't need.

I tap my foot as I consider the possibilities. There's no way I can sneak through a window the way my sisters always do. His windows are always locked and airtight to prevent any leakage of energy. I decide to try the fingerprint scanner. To my surprise, the light above it turns green, and the keypad lights up. I key in the code and the door opens.

I hesitate in the entryway. Is this an invasion of privacy? When my sisters enter my house without my permission, I get irritated. Perhaps I should call him and make an appointment to come around at a different time. I whirl around to depart, but Beckett's voice stops me.

"You heard."

I pivot to address him. "Yes, Jack told me. He also told me the office thinks Brandi is the person you're involved with. What's going on, Beckett?"

He tags my hand and leads me into his living room where he sits on the couch and pulls me onto his lap until I'm straddling him. He wraps his arms around me and buries his head in my chest. I soothe my hands down his back.

"Are you okay?" I ask when he doesn't speak for several minutes.

"I am now," he murmurs before biting my nipple through my blouse.

"Hey!" I slap the side of his head. "Behave."

He sighs before sitting back. "I guess you want to know what happened."

"Can you tell me?"

Board meetings are confidential. I should have considered this before I rushed over here intent on learning the truth. Academically, I know emotions can influence decision-making. I've just never experienced such an impact on my own decision-making until today.

He scoffs. "Of course, I'm going to tell you."

"I didn't ask if you were going to tell me. I asked if you're allowed. If you're not allowed, perhaps I should leave." I attempt to stand but he holds tight to me.

"You're not going anywhere," he grumbles. "And I don't give the first shit if I'm supposed to tell you or not. You are involved in this mess."

Involved in this mess? His words don't offer any comfort.

"Brandi told the Chairman of the Board we're involved."

I gasp. "What? I didn't think she knew."

"She must have walked in on us at some point."

As much as I want to rush off to scold Brandi for intruding on a private moment, there are more important matters to discuss.

"And what did the board decide?"

"Leonard wanted to fire me, but I convinced him the shareholders won't support his decision. We agreed I'll take an unpaid leave of absence until he has a chance to consult with them."

"And what happens when the shareholders agree with his decision?"

He squeezes my arms. "That won't happen."

I scowl. "You don't know what will happen. Answer my question."

"If the shareholders agree with Leonard, he'll fire me."

I gasp and push to my feet. I pace the room as I consider the situation. I don't need to wait for the shareholders' decision. It's obvious what they'll do. Beckett violated the company policy, and he will be punished for his actions.

While I remain unscathed. This doesn't seem fair. I'm as much a participant in this affair as he is. And he's the CEO. This will be a black mark on his record. Finding another CEO position under normal circumstances is difficult. With a black mark on his record, his search will be even more limited.

I, on the other hand, can procure another position as an environmental engineer at any number of firms. There's only one thing to do.

"No," Beckett grumbles.

"No what?"

"I can see the wheels turning in your humongous brain. No."

"Brain sizes are—"

"Stop. You are not using your vast array of knowledge to throw me off the topic. I won't be deterred."

I frown. How does he know I use trivia as a way to change a topic I'm uncomfortable with? "What is the topic?"

"You are not quitting your job."

"It's the most logical course of action."

"Why? Why is it the most logical course of action?"

"I can find another position with ease. There is an abundance of positions for qualified environmental engineers with experience. You, however, are more limited with your job options. There's only one CEO in an engineering company while there are many engineers."

"Give me a chance to solve the situation before you go throwing away your career."

"No. I will not jeopardize your career."

He growls and captures my hands. "And I don't want you jeopardizing your career."

I smile up at him. "This is what love is. Putting someone else's happiness before your own."

"But I'm not happy with this."

I ignore the sting of tears in my eyes and continue, "You'll get over me. You're perfect. You'll find another woman."

He jolts. "Are you breaking up with me?"

"I am," I manage to say despite finding speaking difficult.

His hands tighten. "But we can solve this. I'll talk to the shareholders, and we'll figure it out."

"No. I will not allow you to risk your career for me. I'm not worth it."

His hands move to cradle my face. "You're worth everything to me. I love you."

"And I love you," his eyes light up at my admission, " but I think it's best if we end our relationship before anyone gets hurt."

"You're hurting me now," he whispers; the pain clear to see in his eyes.

My stomach cramps and I fear I will vomit if I don't escape soon. I wrench my hands from his and hurry toward the door.

"I'm not letting you go," he shouts after me.

"I'm afraid you don't have a choice."

"There's always a choice, Lilac. I chose you. You chose me. This will work out."

"I wish I could believe you," I murmur as I shut the door behind me.

I rush to my car and drive away as fast as I can without breaking any speed limits. I need to get home because I'm afraid I'm going to have some sort of breakdown.

I know I did the right thing, but the pain is unbelievable. I never realized emotional pain could hurt as bad as a physical injury. This is not a lesson I'm happy to learn.

Chapter 32

Cheer up – to help someone who is heartbroken and miserable be less miserable by stuffing her full of food and drink while watching movies

I GRUNT WHEN SOMEONE bounces on my bed.

"Leave me alone," I order without bothering to lift my head to check who it is. It's obviously one of my sisters. Anyone else breaking into my apartment wouldn't bother bouncing on the bed.

"Nope. You're heartbroken," Ashlyn says. "We're here to cheer you up."

I lift my head to glare at her. "How do you know?"

"Beckett told us," Cassandra calls from the hallway.

I groan and cover my head with the blanket. "Leave me alone."

Ashlyn rips the blanket away. "Not happening. Sorry. Not sorry."

"Why do you say you're sorry if you're not sorry?"

"It's an expression."

"It's a confusing expression. The whole purpose of an expression—"

pression—"

"Don't change the subject." Ashlyn sniffs. "I think we should force her into the shower before the cheering up portion of the evening can begin."

"Are you experiencing a keener sense of smell?" I frown. "It's appalling how lacking the research regarding pregnant women and their sense of smell is."

"No reason to get on your high horse about the unconscious bias in research studies. Her sense of smell hasn't increased," Juniper says as she strolls into my bedroom. "I think you stink, too."

I lift my t-shirt and sniff it. "I don't smell anything untoward."

"Welp! It's happened. Little Lilac has changed into a real girl."

I glare at Aspen. "I've always been a girl. We took baths together all the time as children. Have you forgotten?"

"I haven't forgotten a thing, but you've obviously forgotten how to clean yourself." She hauls me out of my bed and pushes me toward the bathroom. "Come on. Get in the shower. We'll arrange your cheering up while you clean yourself."

I want to argue with her, but she might have a point. I called in sick to work the day after my confrontation with Beckett and I haven't been back since. It's been three days and I haven't showered, let alone got out of bed.

I should probably be using this experience to study the effect of emotional trauma on a person, but I'm having a hard time caring about science at the moment. I don't think I credited women who were experiencing heartache yet continued to function as adult humans enough in the past.

I quickly shower. I may agree with the need to clean myself, but I am not allowing my sisters to roam around my home unchaperoned for too long.

When I enter the living room, it's stuffed with people. In addition to my sisters, Beckett's sisters are here. I want to tell everyone to go away and leave me to my misery, but I can't. This is the West family ritual.

"What happens now?"

"We need to find what drink is your poison," Ashlyn says.

"I don't want any poison."

"Stop being literal. She means what alcoholic beverage you enjoy when you're depressed," Aspen explains.

"I don't know," I admit. "I don't suffer from depression."

Juniper indicates my body with a flick of her hand. "You're suffering from it now. Unwillingness to bathe and wash your hair are symptoms."

"We can force feed you various drinks until you find one you enjoy," Elizabeth suggests. I raise an eyebrow at her. Force feed? "I mean you can try."

"Fine, but I'm not drinking alone."

"Not it," Aspen, Ashlyn, and Ellery shout at once.

"I'll drink with you," Gabrielle offers.

"But you don't enjoy the taste of alcohol."

I distinctly remember her saying as much when I ate dinner with them at Beckett's house. Beckett. Damn. Everything I think or do seems to remind him of me. Of course, his sisters coming to comfort me doesn't help.

She shrugs. "I could use a bit of cheer in my life."

"What's going on?" Cassandra demands of Gabrielle.

Elizabeth shoves her older sister. "Leave her alone. If she doesn't want to talk about it, you're not going to make her."

Ashlyn rubs her hands together. "And here I was worried we'd be out of the matchmaking business once Lilac is settled."

Gabrielle bristles. "I didn't say anything about a man."

Ashlyn snorts. "Please, if it's not about a man, I'll eat my shirt."

Gabrielle blushes and ducks her chin to hide her face behind her hair.

Elizabeth gasps. "What man is this? What happened?"

Gabrielle shakes her head and shrinks into herself as if she can make herself invisible.

Aspen claps her hands to gain everyone's attention. "One crisis at a time."

"I'm not in crisis," I claim with my attention focused on Gabrielle. I'm more worried about her than myself at the moment.

Aspen fists her hands at her hips. "You haven't been to work in three days and when we arrived, you hadn't showered."

"You can't refute her evidence," Juniper agrees.

"What happened, Lilac? When we had dinner with you last week at Beckett's house, you were both happy and in love." Elizabeth's eyes widen when she realizes what she said. "I mean, I'm not saying you are in love, but you looked it."

"Oh, Beckett's house. What's it like? Is it big? Expensive?" Ashlyn rubs her hands together. "I want all the deets."

Cassandra throws her arm around her shoulders. "I'll tell you all about it later."

"Come on, Lilac," Aspen pleads. "Tell us what happened with Beckett, and I'll run over to *Electric Vibes* and have Lennon make us a couple of pitchers of strawberry margaritas."

"And I'll run over to Rowan's bakery and grab everything he has in vanilla flavor," Ashlyn adds. I didn't realize my sister knew I prefer vanilla over chocolate. What other things does she know about me?

"And I'll grab a bunch of movies for us to watch. Some of which have not yet been released," Juniper offers.

"I can bring Honey over for you to play with," Ellery says after a pause.

Cassandra lifts a bag from the floor. "And I already brought you my homemade salsa and chips."

Elizabeth elbows her. "I'm the one who made the salsa."

Cassandra shrugs. "I bought the ingredients."

I scan their faces and debate lying to them.

Aspen wags her finger at me. "Nope. No lying."

"I don't lie."

"Yes, you do," Juniper insists. "When it's an 'emergency'."

"Heartbreak is definitely an emergency," Gabrielle whispers.

I want to ask her what happened to her, but I know she won't tell me in front of all these women. Plus, Aspen will tackle me if I try to change the topic of discussion. Although, maybe she's pregnant already and won't tackle me. I study her and notice her staring at Ashlyn's belly with envy. Not pregnant yet then.

I inhale a deep breath and count to five before letting it out. "Beckett and I broke up."

"Duh." Ashlyn rolls her eyes. "Why? What happened?"

I don't bother claiming the matter is confidential. They won't care and will pester me until I tell them anyway. "The board wanted to fire him for having a relationship with me, so I quit."

"I'm confused." Elizabeth scratches her head. "Did you quit *and* break up with my brother?"

"Yeah." Ellery's brow furrows. "Why break up with him if you already quit? Doesn't quitting solve the problem?"

I purse my lips. "No. Because Beckett won't accept my resignation unless we're no longer a couple."

"I doubt Beckett will accept your resignation no matter what," Elizabeth mutters.

"What? Why not?"

Elizabeth doesn't get a chance to answer my question as everyone flies into action.

"I'll get the booze!" Aspen shouts before rushing off.

Ashlyn follows her saying, "I'll get the sugary snacks!"

Juniper brings up the rear. "I'll get the movies!"

I stop Ellery before she can leave. "I don't need your puppy to come over."

She sighs. "Good. Because if I return home and Willow sees me, I don't know if I can escape again. I crawled out of the bathroom window to get here the first time."

"Crawled out the window? Your husband isn't keeping you prisoner, is he?" Gabrielle asks.

Ellery rolls her eyes. "No, but my boobs are keeping me chained to my daughter."

Gabrielle relaxes and now I'm seriously concerned about the secret she's hiding.

"Who wants chips and salsa?" Cassandra asks before I have a chance to puzzle out how to ask Gabrielle without embarrassing her.

I notice the tray in Cassandra's hands, and my stomach grumbles in response.

"I figured you hadn't eaten much," she says as she sets the food down on the coffee table in front of me.

I scratch my chin as I contemplate her statement. I can't honestly remember the last time I ate. This has never happened to me before. I remember everything. What's happening to me?

Ellery wraps an arm around me. "It's called heartbreak, but it should be called everything hurts like a bitch."

"For sure," Gabrielle mumbles.

Ellery squeezes my shoulders. "The good news is food, drink, and being around friends helps."

Cassandra plops down on the sofa next to us. "It certainly does." She shoves the tray in my face. "Eat. You'll feel better with a full tummy."

Since concentration loss can be the result of low blood sugar caused by lack of eating, I grab a handful of chips.

My other sisters soon return, and before I know it, I'm watching a humorous film about a group of eleven men who want to rob a casino in Las Vegas. Many of their premises are flawed – eight people carrying 3,600 pounds of one-hundred-dollar bills across a casino floor seems highly unlikely – but overall, the movie is enjoyable.

The movie finishes and I scan this group of women and realize how lucky I am to have them. I also realize they were right. Food, drink, a movie, and some time spent with them did cheer me up.

I still have to face the office on Monday since I have to work through my notice period. And then I have to search for a new job, which will entail moving as Winter Falls is not exactly conveniently located. But with this group at my back, I'm certain I can handle any obstacles I face. Although, I'll have to go on a diet if this is how they're going to cheer me up every time I face an obstacle.

Chapter 33

Stumped – when you can't come up with a means to deal with a problem because you haven't been given all of the relevant information

I HEAR BLEATING AS I walk to the park for Juniper and Maverick's engagement party. One of Phoenix's goats must have escaped again. I dig into my pocket to retrieve my phone to call him, but when I reach the park, I realize no goats have escaped.

"What in the world?" I mumble the question to myself as I scan the baseball field filled with goats and llamas.

"It's a petting zoo," Sage says as she walks over to me.

I normally don't agree with Ashlyn when she calls Juniper an animal freak – the word freak is insulting after all – but in this instance, I can understand where Ashlyn is coming from. Only Juniper would have a petting zoo for her engagement party.

When I turn to address Sage, I realize she's not alone. She's joined by the rest of the gossip gals – Petal, Cayenne, Clove, and Feather. They're wearing bright pink t-shirts with the words *Gossip Gal Party Helper* on them.

"Did Juniper ask you to help out today?"

"She doesn't need to ask for our help. We're always available," Petal says.

"Speaking of which, we need to sort you out."

"What?" I don't know what Sage is referring to. Why would they need to 'sort me out'?

"I'm disappointed. I thought we had this one settled already." Feather sighs.

"I had the candles all wrapped up for her," Petal adds. She owns the candle store, *Sensual Scents*, and makes most of the candles she sells herself.

"I don't think we need to interfere. I think it will all work itself out nicely," Clove says.

"Are you crazy?" Cayenne asks her. "Nothing works itself out without our help."

Perhaps I should escape while they discuss whatever it is they're discussing amongst themselves. They don't seem to need my input.

"Where do you think you're going?" Sage shackles my wrist and pulls me back to the group.

"To congratulate my sister on her engagement."

It's not a lie. If today's event weren't on behalf of my sister and her fiancé I wouldn't be here. Even if I didn't feel as if my heart were breaking into a million pieces, I'd prefer to avoid this party. I do not enjoy social situations. I much prefer to work. But, according to my mother, I am required to attend all social events for the family.

And I do not want to get on my mother's bad side. Her punishments are frightening. The last time I upset her she made me take a dancing class. And not a ballroom dancing class, which I admit could be helpful in the future. No, it was a tango class!

"But we need to sort you out first," Sage yells.

Ellery arrives and drags me away. "Sorry, Sage, family duty calls."

"What family duty?" I ask her once we're out of hearing range of the gossip gals.

"There is no family duty."

"You lied?"

She cocks her eyebrow. "Do you want to go back there and discuss your love life with the gossip gals?"

"My love life? They wanted to discuss my love life with me?"

I don't know why I'm surprised. The gossip gals fancy themselves matchmakers. They believe they're successful as well. Why is unclear to me. As far as I can tell, they didn't assist my sisters with meeting their partners.

"It would have been a short discussion as I currently don't have a love life." My heart clenches and I reach up to rub my chest.

Ellery sighs. "I still don't get why you broke up with Beckett."

"Yeah." Juniper nods in agreement as she joins us along with the rest of my sisters. "If you quit, then there isn't a problem with dating your boss."

"Except I won't live anywhere near White Bridge when I find a new job."

"Wait. What?" Ashlyn screeches. "This is not how the grumpy boss romance books end."

"As I've previously indicated, my life is not a romance book."

She snorts. "Yeah, it is."

"You're going to move away?" Aspen asks with her mouth hanging open.

"I don't think you can criticize me since you lived in Dallas for a decade."

Ellery blows out a puff of air. "And why did she live in Dallas? Because she made a stupid decision about a man, too."

"Are you saying I'm making a stupid decision? You think I should change careers?" I purse my lips. "I've worked entirely too hard to develop my career. I don't plan on changing my career path at this juncture."

"Hold up! Everyone calm down." Juniper waves her arms around as if the motion has the ability to calm people. "There's an easy solution here."

"If you're going to say long-distance relationship, I disagree."

"But Maverick is gone half of the year and we make it work."

"Because Winter Falls is his home base. When I find another job, the location of the job will be my home base. And Beckett's here. A long-distance relationship can only work if one of the people in the relationship is willing to move at a future moment in time, and I can't ask Beckett to move. He's the CEO of the company."

"What about telecommuting?" Ashlyn asks. "The clients I narrate books for are nowhere near Winter Falls."

"I don't think I can supervise the construction of a wind farm or new sewage system from a distance."

"But there must be a solution," Aspen says.

There isn't. I've spent the past week trying to figure out a solution and I've come up empty. If I can't figure out a solution, I don't know how they can. And, since there is no possible solution, I do not wish to speak of the situation any longer.

"Here." I shove the card I bought Juniper at her. "It's a subscription to *National Geographic*. Dr. Blue mentioned you've been stealing his copies."

"Thank you, but I haven't been stealing *National Geographics* from anyone. And I certainly wouldn't steal them from the family doctor of Winter Falls."

"I stole them," Ashlyn admits.

Juniper stares at her. "Why would you steal *National Geographics*?"

"My desk was wobbly and *National Geographic* was the perfect thickness."

Aspen giggles. "Who expected her to say she's been cutting out pictures of naked tribespeople?"

"Why would I cut out pictures of naked people when I have a stud at home who strips for me whenever I ask him to? And I ask him to strip a lot. I'm thinking of having a stripper pole installed in our bedroom. Do you think Cole could handle the construction?"

"Cole is an architect, not a handyman."

"Speaking of Cole." Aspen points across the field to where he's running around the goat enclosure. He appears to be chasing a goat that has fabric hanging out of its mouth. While Cole runs after the animal, Lyric, Rowan, and Maverick shout encouragement.

"Are they cheering on the goat or Cole?" Ashlyn asks.

"I don't care. The goat has Willow's blanket." Ellery marches off to handle things. Ashlyn and Aspen follow her.

"I'll be right there," Juniper hollers after them.

"You should go," I tell her. "You're the animal expert."

She shrugs. "Phoenix is the goat whisperer. Not me." She grasps my hands.

"What are you doing?" I try to tug my hands away, but she holds tight.

"You don't have to stay if you don't want to."

"Yes, I do. This is a family activity. I'm required to stay."

"I promise I won't let Mom make you take a singing class again."

I cringe. The singing class was worse than the tango class.

"Thank you, but I should stay."

"But I hate seeing you this way."

This way? Do I not look okay? I glance down at the dress I'm wearing. It's a simple sundress, but I think it fits my figure nicely.

She squeezes my hands. "The dress is lovely. I mean how sad you are."

"I'm not sad. I'm happy to celebrate your engagement with you."

"You're lying again." I have no response since she's correct. I need to make a note of how heartbreak leads a person to compromising their values. "I hate this part of the process."

"What process?"

"The mating process."

I yank my hands from hers and cross my arms over my chest. "This is not part of the mating process. You're mistaken. Beckett and I are over." I demonstrated how there is no solution to our situation not five minutes ago.

She pats my shoulder. "Yeah. Uh-huh."

I frown at her hand on my shoulder. "Why are you placating me?"

"Because if I tell you you're wrong, you'll begin a discussion on how you're never wrong. Except, in this instance, you are wrong."

"In this instance, I don't think I would mind being proven wrong," I mutter. This is a most unusual statement for me as I do hate to be wrong.

Tap. Tap. Tap. "Can I have everyone's attention?"

What in the world is Beckett doing here, and why is he standing on the stage?

"Someone's about to be proven wrong," Juniper sings as she drags me to the stage.

Ashlyn, Aspen, and Ellery join us as do Beckett's sisters.

"What's going on?" I ask Gabrielle as I know Cassandra or Elizabeth won't tell me.

She smiles. "You'll see."

Chapter 34

Grand gesture – when a man makes an especially elaborate and showy action to win his girlfriend back

BECKETT

I tap on the microphone to make sure it's on. "Can I have everyone's attention?"

My gaze is focused on Lilac, so I don't miss how she jumps upon hearing my voice. I'm afraid she's going to try and run away, but her sister drags her to a spot in front of the stage where she's joined by her other sisters and mine.

She asks Gabrielle what's happening, and I smile when my youngest sister refuses to answer. Of course, my sisters don't know what I did any more than Lilac does.

"I have an announcement."

"And? Are you going to keep up in suspense all day?" Ashlyn shouts at me.

Her husband, Rowan, kisses her hair before whispering something to her. She melts into him, and I try not to be jealous of their relationship. Soon, I promise myself. Soon, Lilac and I will be a loving couple again.

"I want to announce the appointment of the Chief Technical Officer at *Clean Mountain Environment*."

"Why are you announcing a new appointment to the company at Juniper's engagement party?" Lilac asks.

Her sisters giggle at her confusion.

"This is the equivalent of a nerd grand gesture," Maverick says.

"We did tell him to do a grand gesture when the time is right," Lyric points out, and Rowan and Cole nod in agreement.

The gossip gals elbow their way to the front. "Go ahead, Beckett." Sage motions for me to continue.

"Why do the gossip gals know what's happening?" Lilac asks.

Juniper pats her arm. "It's part of the mating ritual."

Lilac frowns at her. "You, of all people, should realize mating ritual refers to procreative behavior in animals."

"This is procreative behavior. Courtship display falls under procreative behavior."

"Beckett, please say what you have to say before these two nerds cause everyone in the audience to fall into a nerd-coma. I'm begging you." Ashlyn puts her hands together as if in prayer and bats her eyelashes at me.

"Nerd-coma isn't a thing," Lilac tells her.

Ashlyn pretends to faint, and when Rowan catches her, she begins snoring.

"What's going on? What did we miss?" Lilac's Mom asks as she and her dad join the crowd.

Her hair is disheveled and her dad's wearing a shit-eating grin.

"Where have you been?" Lilac asks despite the obvious answer.

Ashlyn feigns gagging. "No. I don't want to know."

Lilac lifts an eyebrow. "Told you nerd-coma wasn't a real affliction."

Aspen motions to the stage. "Beckett is trying to do a grand gesture."

"A nerd grand gesture," Lyric clarifies.

"But my sisters won't shut up long enough for him to make his announcement," Cassandra says.

"I haven't said a word." Elizabeth's nose wrinkles. "Except I did say five words. Oh wait, now it's more."

Cassandra snorts. "Awkward girl strikes again."

Ruby frowns at her. "We don't use the word awkward in reference to a person," she scolds.

Cassandra's cheeks darken and she mumbles, "Sorry."

"Can I announce who the new CTO is now?" I ask before they start another inane conversation.

Lilac motions for me to carry on. "Go ahead, although I still don't understand why you're doing this at Juniper and Maverick's engagement petting zoo."

"My wedding circus celebration was better," Ashlyn claims.

So much for them not getting into another inane conversation.

"I asked Maverick permission to make an announcement. Now—"

"What?" Ashlyn's screech cuts me off. "Maverick knows what your grand gesture is. No fair." She gazes up at her husband. "Do you know?"

I tap on the microphone to gain her attention. "Maverick doesn't know what I'm going to say."

She wags her finger at me. "You don't know how lucky you are. You'd look good with a clown face."

"You can't break into his house. He has a biometric locking mechanism," Lilac tells her.

"Challenge accepted!"

Shit. I make a mental note to have the security company come out next week to review the security on my house.

I tap on the microphone again. This time I don't ask if I can announce anything. I just go ahead and say it.

"I'd like to congratulate Lilac West on her new position as CTO of *Clean Mountain Environment.*"

"Whoo-hoo!" Juniper waves her arms around in a victory dance. "I knew you'd prove Lilac wrong."

Lilac appears adorably confused. "But I quit my position with the company."

"And now you have a new position."

"But…" She flaps her arms like their wings.

I jump off the stage and walk to her. I cup her chin. "This way we can be together."

"Who had today as the proposal date?" Sage shouts, and I realize we're standing in the middle of a crowd.

I release her face and tag her hand before drawing her away from the rush of people. When I stop at the tennis court, Lilac shakes her head.

"You need to go further if you want to get away from them." She indicates the crowd following behind us.

"Where do you suggest?"

"My place."

"Boo!" Feather yells. "How are we supposed to eavesdrop? She lives on the second floor."

"She has a balcony," Ashlyn says.

Rowan growls. "You are not climbing on Lilac's balcony."

"Come on." I drag her to my car.

I'm relieved when no one follows us. Of course, no one else has a car here. Besides Lilac, I haven't met another Winter Falls resident who owns a car.

"Turn here," Lilac says when I head in the direction of her apartment.

I don't bother asking her where we're going and follow her directions. I park in a small lot and turn to Lilac but she's already exiting the car. When I open the door to follow her, I hear the sound of running water. We must be at the falls for which Winter Falls is named.

"They'll never expect us to go somewhere in nature. They think I hate nature."

"You don't hate nature. Your whole career is premised on saving nature." It amazes me how little Lilac's family and friends understand her. Especially since she's not difficult to under-stand.

I grasp her hand as we begin to walk. When she doesn't pull away, I consider it a good sign. We reach a clearing on top of the falls and stop.

"Now, let's discuss this without everyone listening in," she says and pulls away from me.

"What's there to discuss?"

"What's there to discuss?" she repeats. "How about you giving me a position because we're involved?"

"One." I hold up a finger. "We weren't involved when you were elected by the board for the position since you had broken up with me."

"Two." I hold up a second finger. "I didn't give you the position. You were elected by the board."

"But how? I applied for the position over a year ago and was turned down."

I shrug. "Perhaps the board felt you were a better fit now than you were a year ago."

She narrows her eyes on me. "What aren't you telling me?"

A lot. But how much will she accept of the truth?

"The shareholders wanted you to be given the position."

"The shareholders? But I don't know any of the shareholders."

Here comes the tricky part. "Actually, you do."

Her nose scrunches as she puzzles it out in her head. I'm not surprised when she nods.

"Of course. It makes sense. I should have realized. When did you become the majority shareholder?"

"Last year before I took the position of CEO."

Her lips purse. "Aspen was right when she claimed you were wealthy." I nod. "How much is your net worth?"

I shrug. "My parents left us a nice nest egg when they passed." Her eyes widen in surprise, but I don't want to talk about money. "Now, about your new position."

She scowls. "I don't understand how you as the majority shareholder made a board decision."

"I didn't. The majority of the board – Stan, Doris, Norman, and myself – all voted for you." I don't tell her Leonard tried to veto the vote. He won't be in his position much longer anyway. "Have I satisfactorily answered your questions?"

"Yes, I believe you have."

"Good." I draw her near, but before my lips can meet hers, she stops me.

"What are you doing?"

"I'm going to make out with the woman I love for a while before I take her home and make love to her."

"I haven't agreed to rekindle our relationship."

"Honey, you love me and the only reason you broke up with me was because of our work situation. The work situation is sorted."

"I know, but I thought we had to verbally agree to restart our relationship."

"I agree. Now, can I kiss you? I've missed you this past week."

"I missed you, too."

"And now you're mine."

"Only forever," she whispers before my lips find hers and the talking portion of our day is finished.

Chapter 35

Wrong – when your head is so far up your ass you can't see what's right in front of you

"Are you going to chase after them?" I ask Ellery as we stand watching Beckett and Lilac drive off.

"Nah. We were only giving her a hard time."

"I wasn't *only* giving her a hard time," Ashlyn declares. "But big guy here won't let me go in pursuit."

"It's Juniper and Maverick's engagement party," Rowan reminds her. "You should stay here and celebrate with them."

She motions toward the end of the baseball field where the engaged couple is sneaking off. "I don't think Juniper and Maverick are going to be around for much longer."

He tries another tactic to distract her. "I thought you wanted to play with the foxes?"

"Holy cow! Have you seen them? They're the most adorable foxes in the world with their gigantic ears. Let's go pet them."

She yanks on her husband's hand and tugs him toward the enclosure for the foxes.

"I better go check on Willow," Ellery says and walks off leaving me alone with my sisters.

"I wish Olivia were here," I say.

Cassandra frowns. "Why? So she can ruin Beckett's day?"

"She doesn't ruin things on purpose."

She snorts. "You're so naïve," she says before she pets the top of my head like I'm a doll and walks off.

Elizabeth wraps her arm around my shoulder. "Don't listen to her. She's just jealous of Beckett and Lilac."

"Now," one of the elderly ladies wearing a t-shirt with the words *Gossip Gal Party Helper* on it says as she joins us, "we have a list for you."

"Excuse me? Who are you?"

She gestures toward the group of women with her. "We're the women who are going to fulfill all your wishes."

All my wishes? Can she rid me of my shyness and make me not afraid of my own shadow?

"Are you a genie? I don't see your bottle." Elizabeth pretends to search the ground for a bottle.

"We're not genies," says another woman. "We're the best dang matchmakers this town has ever seen."

"And I have a list of possible matches for you." The first woman waves a piece of paper in the air. "First off, Phoenix."

At the name Phoenix, my heart increases, and my belly dips. The goat farmer is gorgeous with a capital G. Plus, he's gentle with his animals. I might have a bit of a crush on him.

"Phoenix doesn't want to be matched," I tell them.

"Which is why we should match him first."

"He should know better than to think he can tell us what to do."

While the women bicker amongst themselves, Elizabeth pushes me behind her. "Go," she whispers. "Escape. I'll hold them off."

I rush off before the ladies realize I'm leaving. I'm drawn to the enclosure with the goats. I wonder if Pan is here, although I'm not sure I'd recognize her.

I open the gate and step into the grassy area. A goat immediately rushes to me and bites down on my skirt. "And here I thought I wouldn't recognize you. How are you, Pan?"

I pet her for a few seconds before I decide I better free my skirt or I'll end up walking home in my panties. Gosh, no. I pull on the fabric, but Pan isn't relinquishing her hold.

"Come on, Pan. Let go. You don't want me to go home naked, do you?"

The goat is unaffected by my pleas. I scan the enclosure for anyone who can help and my gaze lands on Phoenix. I pause to watch him walk away from me. His butt was made for wearing those jeans. It fills out the worn fabric to perfection.

"Phoenix," I cry out, but he doesn't hear me.

Great. I have to drag a goat with me across a field. At least no one's around to see me as most of the crowd has now migrated to the picnic tables near the barbeque.

"We're going for a walk, Pan," I say as I start toward where Phoenix is.

I hope Pan will let go of my skirt as we go, but the goat has no problem chomping away on my skirt and walking at the same time. Figures.

"Hey," I shout as I approach Phoenix, but he doesn't hear me and rounds the pen out of my view.

"Oh, hey, Lyric," Phoenix says, and I stop. I don't want to intrude.

"Hey, little brother."

"What's up?"

"Not much. Have you seen Beckett's sisters? They're a pretty bunch."

"What are you? A member of the gossip gals matchmakers now?"

"Nah. But the youngest one, Gabrielle, seems to have a crush on you."

I cringe. How did Lyric notice? I didn't think I was being obvious.

"Gabrielle's nice."

I cringe. Nice is a death knoll.

"But I'm not looking for a relationship now."

"You need to get over her." Her? Who's her?

"I'm over her."

"Which is why you're running scared when a nice girl like Gabrielle's interested."

"Gabrielle's soft. She could never handle life on the farm anyway."

I slam a hand over my mouth before anyone can hear me gasp. Soft. If nice is bad, soft is worse. Much worse.

"Your loss."

I hear someone moving closer. Shoot. Shoot. What do I do? I try to run away, but Pan is still latched onto my skirt.

"Stop it, Pan!" I yank at my skirt, and it rips.

I don't wait to check how bad the rip is. I take off running.

"Gabrielle!" Phoenix calls my name, but I don't turn around. I'm sure my face is the color of an overripe tomato by now.

I'm such an idiot. Why would I think Phoenix could ever like me?

D. E. Haggerty
Love and Laughter in Every Chapter

D.E. Haggerty is an American who has spent the majority of her adult life abroad. She has lived in Istanbul, various places throughout Germany, and currently finds herself in The Hague. She has been a military policewoman, a lawyer, a B&B owner/operator and now a writer.